URCELIA TEIXEIRA

faith-filled mystery & suspense

"THE LIGHT SHINES IN THE DARKNESS,
AND THE DARKNESS HAS NOT
OVERCOME IT."

— JOHN 1:5

# HANNAH'S HALO

**A THRILLING CHRISTIAN MYSTERY NOVEL**

**ANGUS REID MYSTERIES - BOOK IV**

# URCELIA TEIXEIRA

AWARD WINNING AUTHOR

HANNAH'S HALO

A THRILLING CHRISTIAN MYSTERY NOVEL

ANGUS REID MYSTERIES BOOK IV

URCELIA TEIXEIRA

# CONTENTS

*To my daughter, Hannah,*

*Thank you for letting me use your name to be a part of this story.*
*Your life is a shining testimony to achieving success the Godly way!*
*May your path always be blessed, and your dreams divinely guided!*

INSPIRED BY

"For where you have envy and selfish ambition, there you find disorder and every evil practice."

James 3:16
(NIV)

# PREFACE

Hannah Jackson had no idea that the darkness she sought to expose would soon turn against her. Ambition had led her to this moment, blinding her to the danger that lurked just beneath the surface, waiting to ensnare her. In the shadows of her own aspirations, she was about to discover that some truths are far more perilous than the secrets they uncover.

As Hannah plunged into the dark heart of Weyport with a relentless ambition pushing her to unveil every buried secret, a chilling sense of danger loomed ever closer. She navigated through shadowy alleyways and whispered rumors, driven by an insatiable hunger for the truth. Each revelation felt like a victory, but with every step forward, an invisible noose tightened around her. Unbeknownst to her, the chaos she sought to expose was silently closing in, ensnaring her in its deadly grip.

Envy and selfish ambition weren't just the focus of her investigation; they were the sinister forces stalking her every step, poised to devour her whole. The deeper she dug, the more she realized that these dark desires weren't confined to the stories she pursued—they were embedded within the very fabric of Weyport, and perhaps, within herself. As Hannah's quest for truth spiraled into a fight for survival, she had to confront not only the shadows of the town, but also the darkness within her own soul.

The lines between hunter and hunted blurred, and Hannah found herself caught in a deadly game where the stakes were nothing less than her own life.

Welcome to Weyport, where every secret comes at a price, and every revelation might be your last.

# CHAPTER ONE

S he stared at the pair of aces in her hand, then glanced up at the two men beside her at the poker table. Her heart pounded against her ribcage, her insides trembling as she scrutinized their faces. They were the final two players, whittled down from the usual eight she contended against every week. The prize: a seat at the elite players' table in the high-stakes Dragon Room at The Grande—and a chance to get close to her target.

A faint smile threatened to spread across her face, but she maintained a straight face. This was the first time she had made it to the final round since she began her investigation nearly a year ago. It was the closest she'd come to getting inside the belly of the beast.

And the stakes were higher than ever.

In the dim, smoke-filled room hidden behind the Turkish barbershop on the far side of town, she glanced at her opponents' stone faces before her eyes dropped back to the cards in her hands. Anxiety gnawed at her insides. If she lost this hand, she was out of the tournament. Three more months of tireless effort would be in vain. Another opportunity wasted, and she'd have to start all over again. She was running out of time and patience. So was her editor. If she let this opportunity slip through her fingers, she'd be back at square one. She couldn't afford another dead end. Not again. Not tonight. She needed to make tonight count. With every game she played, the risk of her true identity being discovered grew. It was a risk she had long accepted, willing to face any danger if it meant breaking the biggest news story of her career.

A small voice in the back of her mind whispered a warning. The stakes were high, too high, and she was way out of her depth. If she had any sense, she'd fold and get out of there. Trust her instincts. Let go of her dreams and the career for which she was so desperately fighting.

Yet she couldn't. She was too close. She'd come too far and had given up too much to run scared now.

Another voice echoed in her head. A more persistent one. Her father's.

"You don't have what it takes, Princess. Marry rich and leave it to us men to do the real jobs."

Frustration threatened to spill onto her face at the flashing memory of their recent conversation. She was used to her father's chauvinistic remarks. He'd made his opinion of women abundantly clear since the day her mother left them. She was only ten at the time, far too young to understand his hatred toward all women. Not anymore. Now his ridicule fueled her, pushed her to work harder so she could finally get out of Weyport. Though her father's anger toward her mother projected onto her and should have ruined her life, it only made her more determined than ever to prove him wrong. She was destined for greatness, regardless of her being a woman or the result of a failed multiracial marriage. Another detail he constantly brought up, as if the color of her skin was somehow a deficit to her ability to succeed.

She pushed the negative emotions aside, straightened her back, and found her nerve again. This wasn't the time to get distracted, least of all by her father's condescending opinions. If she were to finally make it to the big leagues in New York, she had to keep her head in the game. These guys were professionals. They'd smell a charlatan from a mile away. If she showed the slightest hesitation or dropped her guard, her cover would be blown, taking nearly twelve months of work down the drain with it.

Her scalp itched under the wavy brown wig she wore to hide her identity. She absentmindedly scratched at the spot with a long, red fingernail—another accessory along with the false eyelashes and six-inch heels she wore to look the part. It was what was necessary to get behind the curtain.

Warmth flushed into her chest. She was so close to success she could almost taste it. The mix of fear and excitement churned within her, a volatile cocktail of emotions that kept her on edge, but also sharpened her focus. She couldn't afford to mess this up—not when so much was on the line.

She took a deep breath, feeling the weight of the room pressing down on her. The smoke hung thick in the air, mixing with the scent of sweat and cheap cologne, creating an oppressive atmosphere that made it hard to breathe. Every eye in the room was on her, waiting for her next move. She could feel the pressure building, threatening to crush her.

Hannah glanced at the clock on the wall. Time seemed to slow down, each tick on the second hand echoing in her ears like a drumbeat. She had to make a decision, and she had to make it now. The voices in her head battled for dominance — her father's taunts mixing with her own doubts and fears. She pushed them all aside, deciding to focus instead on her opponents' unspoken strategies.

Across from her, a regular out-of-towner's eyes narrowed as he studied her face. A chubby, slimy, cigar-smoking, middle-aged man who always came dressed in a shiny silver suit, wearing far too many chunky rings like he was channeling Liberace. She had no interest in finding out who he really was or where he came from— he wasn't the subject of her investigation. But he was annoying. A thorn in her side who had managed to knock her out of nearly every game since she started. She wanted to roll her eyes at the greaseball and snap a witty remark, but she forced her attention back to her mission and the cards in her hand. She had lost her concentration, played straight into his tactics, and allowed her mind to drift from the game. That could cost her everything.

Desperate to refocus and maintain her cover, she placed her cards face down on the forest green velveteen-covered table. One hand absently toyed with the poker chips in front of her while the other reached for her drink, a facade of calm amidst the tension.

"Getting too hot in the kitchen for you, sweetheart?" the greaseball taunted as she put her glass of gin back in its place.

Steady now, Hannah.

Her voice was controlled when she spoke.

"I could ask you the same question, Mr. Roxworthy. Your leg hasn't stopped twitching since we started this hand."

She cocked her head and narrowed her eyes, putting him in his place. Then she pinched one corner of her cards to peek at her hand before dropping them back in place. Inside, her nerves were shot. On the outside, there was no trace of it. Somehow, she had managed to keep her head together and hide the knots twisting her stomach into an even tighter ball. A small feat she inwardly celebrated. For once, she had played him at his own game.

Mr. Roxworthy's face turned a deep red when the

player next to him snickered with amusement, but he ignored it. He knew better.

Jack Travis, her other opponent, smiled at Hannah, then lifted his crystal glass in her direction. His encouraging gesture sent butterflies into her stomach—not the good kind. The kind that hinted at the evil lurking behind his sheepish grin.

There was nothing nice about Jack Travis. His friendly smile was as fake as the counterfeit Rolex on his wrist and the knock-off Armani suit he thought had everyone fooled.

But like his cheap cologne that clung to the air in the small private gambling room, so did his dark presence. A presence that warned he wasn't to be challenged.

# CHAPTER TWO

I n the shadows behind Jack, his entourage stood like silent waiters, the slight bulges under their black windbreakers revealing that they were armed. "Sin protectors" she liked to call them. Men who pledged allegiance to their employer's evil crimes. Wrongdoings she was determined to expose to the world as soon as she pieced it all together. Jack Travis would be revealed when she took down the man he was working for. For now, she needed to keep cool, keep her eye on the big shark, and win this round.

Hannah's eyes met Jack's, and she forced her red-stained lips into a smile. The butterflies in her stomach quickly morphed into a pulsating tension in her lower back. She straightened her posture. She was playing a dangerous game, but if she were to get the evidence she needed to blow their entire operation out of the water, this was the only way. She needed to gain Jack's trust, get up close, personal even if that was what it took. He was her only way in—and her only way out of Weyport.

Jack smiled back at her. The slimy intentions behind his eyes pushed revolt into the back of her throat. She forced it down with a swig of her drink, the burn of the alcohol helping to steady her nerves.

"Play or fold. I ain't got all night, sweetheart," Roxworthy challenged, his leg now dead still beneath the table.

Don't bite, Hannah. Remember why you're here.

Mr. Roxworthy's already pronounced bottom jaw pushed out even more as his bushy eyebrows lifted, prompting her to hurry up. The smoke from his cigar curled upward, creating a haze that added to the oppressive atmosphere.

Hannah placed her glass back atop the mahogany table's overhang, aware that two of Jack's men were speaking in quiet murmurs at the back of the room. She was about to add a few more poker chips to the already high pile in the middle of the table when one of Jack's men leaned in over his shoulder and whispered something in his ear.

Dropping her gaze to pretend-study her cards, Hannah tried to eavesdrop. When she couldn't hear what he was saying, she looked up and tried to read his lips. Roxworthy puffed a thick cloud of cigar smoke in her direction, taunting her to try to throw her off her game.

Her gaze locked with his, the spiteful glimmer in his eyes mocking her to react.

A moment later, Jack slammed his cards down hard on the table, causing his nearby drink to splatter droplets of golden liquid all over the table. Roxworthy startled, nearly swallowing his cigar in the process.

Abruptly standing, Jack bumped the table, causing his small tower of poker chips to tumble into a messy pile.

Whatever his sidekick had just told him instantly transformed his face into an expression fueled by pure evil. The way he looked at her warned that she might be at the heart of his fury.

Roxworthy must have seen it too, his face revealing panic that was made worse when Jack noisily shoved his chair to the ground with the back of his knees.

"Hey, watch it!" Roxworthy finally had the nerve to snap when Jack's elbow knocked into him, spilling half his beverage all over his rounded midsection.

But Jack showed little concern. His eyes were lit with rage as they locked onto Hannah's face, sending shivers down her spine.

Jack turned to leave without saying a word.

Speak up, Hannah! Stop him! The little voice in her head prompted.

"Anything the matter, Mr. Travis?" she blurted out without thinking, annoyed with herself for not coming up with something more original.

Not that it would have mattered. That much was

evident when Jack responded by glancing back at her, his eyes even darker. So chilling was his stare that Hannah could feel the blood in her veins freeze under the hate and anger radiating from his gaze. Her breath caught in the back of her throat, and she fought hard to keep the fear contained. To her relief, Jack spun back around and instead moved toward the exit.

"Hey, you can't just up and leave, Travis! This isn't a high school game under the bleachers, you know," Roxworthy barked as he watched one of Jack's men gather his boss' winnings, his cold eyes warning Roxworthy to back off.

But Roxworthy was like a pit bull and didn't let go. He jumped up, pointing a pudgy index finger in Jack's direction.

"Travis! You might be calling the shots around here, but that doesn't make this right!"

Before Roxworthy could say another word, the henchman next to him pushed him back down into his seat then turned and followed after his boss.

"It's late. I have to get going anyway," Hannah quickly announced as she pushed herself away from the table. It was the excuse she needed to follow Jack. Her gut told her that something big must have gone down for him to forfeit the game. And that meant opportunity. She couldn't let it slip. No way.

"A bunch of cowards, you are," Roxworthy spat. "There are going to be penalties for this, you hear me? I'll make sure of it!" he yelled before finishing what was left in his glass. As Hannah turned to grab her coat from the back of her chair, Roxworthy leaned across the table to sneak a look at the cards she had left face down. But the dealer's hand stopped him before he could turn them over.

"There's always next week, Mr. Roxworthy," Hannah yelled over her shoulder as she hurried after Jack.

"Losers!" he yelled after them.

Once outside the room, Hannah quickened her pace down the dim corridor that led to the exit and the alleyway behind the Turkish barbershop. She burst through the exit door and into the quiet, dark street, pausing briefly as her eyes searched the shadows. There was no sign of Jack Travis or his men. She was too late. Jack had already vanished into the quiet of the night.

She hurried toward the top of the narrow street, careful not to break her ankles in the black heels she hated wearing. She cursed out loud, sending an echo down the narrow backstreet toward the road where she had parked her car around the corner. Her mind raced with thoughts of what could have caused Jack to leave so abruptly. Was it possible he found out who she really was?

A sudden noise came from somewhere behind. She snapped around to find it, slamming into a man's muscled torso feeling as if she had walked into a brick wall. She stumbled back from the impact, dropping her coat and nearly twisting her ankle in the process.

Strong hands wrapped around her biceps, pinching

the tender folds of her bare skin. She squealed at the sudden discomfort and lost complete control over her body when, in one quick motion, the man pinned her against the cold brick wall behind her. Pain turned to fear, and the sudden hard impact left her dizzy and gasping to find her breath.

When she looked up, she stared straight into the deadly eyes of one of Jack Travis's sidekicks.

# CHAPTER THREE

His grip tightened, and she could see the menace in his expression. The man's breath was hot against her face as he leaned in closer.

"Think you're clever, don't you?" he hissed, his voice low and threatening. "Mr. Travis doesn't like being played."

"I wasn't..." Hannah tried to protest, but the words caught in her throat. The man's grip tightened further, cutting off her air supply momentarily.

"Save it," he growled.

Hannah's pulse quickened. What would they do to her now that she was caught? Her instincts screamed at her to fight back, but her body felt paralyzed with fear.

"What are you doing? Let go, you're hurting me!" she wrestled to break loose from his grip.

But instead, he tightened his grip even more to the

point where she thought her arms were going to snap in two. Tears spilled over onto her cheeks as the voice in her head now shouted, "I told you so!"

For the briefest of moments, she thought of kicking him in the shin, or jamming her knee where he was most vulnerable. But even if either action had the desired effect, she'd never be able to outrun the five men behind him.

Moments later, Jack spoke to his goons from the shadows, the now familiar scent of his cheap cologne burning her nostrils as she kept up the struggle.

"Let me go!" she squirmed.

From the darkness, Jack moved into view, his eyes as cold as they were when he looked at her in the poker room.

"What are you doing? Tell him to let me go or I'll scream!"

"Yeah, you don't want to do that, Ellie. Or shall I call you Hannah Jackson?"

Her stomach dropped like lead into her legs. He had found out who she was. What else did he know?

"So what? I'd be a fool to use my real name in an underground poker game," she bluffed, still wrestling to break free.

He grunted like a wolf around its prey.

"Except we both know you're not here for the love of the game."

"Why else?" Panic ripped through her body as she wrestled to free her arms that were still caught in his minion's strong grip.

Jack bellowed a sadistic laugh so loud it ricocheted off the brick wall behind her.

"I'm no fool, Miss Jackson. Don't toy with me."

"I'm not! I need the money."

He grunted then turned to face another one of his men.

"Throw her in the trunk until I know what to do with her."

"What? No!" Hannah cried out as she wrestled against the man's strong hold.

"Let me go! You have no right to do this. This is assault!"

But Travis ignored her weak threat and set off toward the black Bentley that stood parked in the middle of the dark alley.

"Let go of me! Help!" she screamed.

The man whose big hands cut into her flesh moved to throw her over one shoulder.

Hannah screamed louder, but her cry for help was brought to an abrupt stop when the back of her keeper's big hand whipped across her face.

She squealed, the impact of the beating leaving behind a vicious burn and a dizzy spell.

Blood pooled in her mouth, and she spat it into her assailant's face.

"You won't get away with this, Travis!" she fought on, kicking and screaming for help before another backhand slapped across the other cheek.

This time it nearly knocked her out.

"Tape her trap shut before you toss her in!" Jack shouted from the car.

Barely conscious, Hannah kept wrestling. If the man succeeded with getting her in the trunk, she was done for. She'd seen it on the Oprah show once. But the man was much stronger than her, and before she knew it, he had picked up her ninety-pound body with ease. Tucked under his arm like a football, his other hand firmly clamped over her mouth and nose, he carried her to the Bentley.

But Hannah didn't quit. If there was one thing Hannah Jackson knew, it was to fight back. So, when he tried to open the trunk, she wedged her feet up onto the rear of the car and pushed her body back against his.

Needing both his hands to force her into the trunk, he let go of her mouth and she let out a loud scream she was certain would be heard all the way through town.

In the distance, a car's tires screeched.

She kept fighting, kept pushing her legs against the Bentley's taillight as much as her small frame would allow.

"Shut her up!" Jack yelled from inside the vehicle, prompting two more of his men to rush to his command.

The men moved toward her, and she drove her stiletto heel into one of the henchmen's thighs, sending him back and squealing in pain. With one more shove of her legs against the tailgate, she managed to send her handler off balance, pulling her to the ground with him.

She scrambled in one final attempt to get away but couldn't, so she screamed for help once more.

Determined to finish the job, the other man cursed at her then drove his fist into her jaw, the blow instantly rendering her helpless on the ground and unable to fight back.

Moments later, a car's bright lights pierced through the darkness, its headlights illuminating the ghastly scene.

Tires screeched behind them, followed by the deafening sound of the approaching car's horn.

Weak and barely conscious, Hannah tried to peel herself off the ground.

Jack yelled at his men, their panicked voices blending into the chaos.

The car's horn blared incessantly.

There was a scurry of feet around her.

Doors slammed.

More screeching tires.

Then everything went black.

# CHAPTER FOUR

Hannah's eyes fluttered open, and she winced at the blinding fluorescent lights above her. The antiseptic smell of the hospital hit her first, followed by a dull throbbing in her head and jaw. Groaning softly, she blinked away the haze and looked around.

Insipid magnolia hues adorned the walls, neatly paired with the single half-drawn curtain next to her bed. The rhythmic beeping of the heart monitor and the distant murmur of hospital activity told her where she was. She tried to move but was met with a sharp pain in her ribs. It took a moment for her memory to catch up. The Turkish barber shop, the poker game's abrupt ending, the back alley, the beating she received at the hands of Jack Travis's men, and then darkness.

"You're awake." A stern voice cut through her foggy

thoughts. Hannah turned her head, the movement sending waves of pain through her body, to see her editor, Clara Matthews, sitting by her bedside. Clara's glasses perched on the bridge of her nose, her expression a mixture of relief and anger.

"Clara?" Hannah croaked, her throat dry and raspy.

"Yes, it's me," Clara said, her voice tight with controlled frustration. "Do you have any idea how much trouble you're in?"

Hannah attempted a small nod, which only made her head spin. "I—I'm sorry. I had to keep going. I'm so close."

Clara's eyes narrowed.

"I told you not to chase after this story. It's too danger-ous. Now look at you. You're lucky to be alive."

Hannah swallowed, her mouth feeling like sandpaper.

"What happened? How did I get here?"

Clara sighed, the anger giving way to concern.

"Someone found you in that alley behind the Turkish barbershop. They brought you here, didn't want to leave their name. The nurses said they had covered their face with one of those COVID masks. A Good Samaritan, the doctors said. Do you remember anything about it?"

Hannah frowned, trying to recall. She remembered the blows, the fear, the helplessness, and then...nothing.

"No, I don't. I didn't see anyone. Just Jack Travis's men."

Clara shook her head.

"This isn't a game, Hannah. You could have been killed. The poker game, the underground tournament, all of it was reckless."

"I know," Hannah whispered, her determination undiminished despite the pain. "But I'm closer now than ever before, Clara. I just need a bit more time."

Clara's head shook before she'd even finished her sentence.

"Forget it, Hannah. I'm pulling you off this story. It's not worth getting killed over."

Hannah pushed her bruised body upright, fighting nausea as her head spun.

"You can't do that, Clara. I've been working this story for the better part of a year and I'm one game away from getting to the Dragon Room. Please! I just need a little more time. I'm fine. I can finish this."

Judging by Clara's single raised eyebrow, Hannah knew her editor wasn't convinced. Clara confirmed this by shaking her head even more and standing up.

"There's not going to be another game, Hannah. Jack Travis is a dangerous man. You've experienced it yourself, for goodness' sake! There's a reason he tried to do who knows what to you. Count yourself lucky you didn't end up dead behind the dumpsters. Uh-uh, not happening. Not on my watch."

"I'm not after him," Hannah argued.

"He doesn't know that though, does he?" Clara's hands

were on her hips. "It's very obvious he knows who you are now, Hannah. He's not going to let that go."

"I know, but maybe if I try another angle—"

"Like what? By now Travis has already given Duncan Steele the heads-up, and trust me honey, no disguise will fool the master of fake. The best we can do for now is let the dust settle and hope they slip up somewhere."

Hannah's gaze drifted to a spot on the wall. She couldn't stop now. She'd worked too hard. This was her chance to prove her father wrong about her; it was her one ticket out of this stupid town.

She reached for the plastic tumbler with water next to her bed, took a sip, then looked up at Clara.

"I need to find out who helped me. They might know something we don't. If I can just talk to them, find out why they helped me. It could be a break in the case." She ignored Clara's defensive body language. "What if this Good Samaritan had evidence to substantiate the claims, proof that they're rigging the machines? That's all we need to go to the sheriff and open an investigation, Clara. Imagine what this story would do for the paper, for your career!"

Clara exhaled sharply, her no-nonsense demeanor returning.

"You need to drop this story, rest, and recover. This obsession with The Grande is going to get you killed. Trust me honey, chasing fame and fortune isn't all it's cracked up to be."

"I can't stop now," Hannah said, her voice stronger. "There's too much at stake. Weyport needs to know the truth about what's happening at that casino. They're being swindled out of their retirement funds, their life savings. We can't just let it go, Clara."

Clara studied her for a moment, then sighed.

"You're as stubborn as they come, Hannah Jackson."

Hannah tried to smile, wincing when the cut on her lip stopped her from doing so.

"Fine," Clara started. "But I'm forbidding you to go anywhere near the poker games and Jack Travis. You stay away from the barbershop and turn your attention to finding the person who saved you. Got it? We'll take the Good Samaritan angle instead."

Hannah's eyes lit up, her mind racing. The mysterious savior, the brutal attack, the secrets she had yet to uncover —they all swirled together, fueling her resolve. Finding out who saved her and why might just be the key to unraveling the entire mystery at The Grande.

"And promise me you'll be more careful. I don't want to lose one of my best reporters," Clara's voice cut through her thoughts.

Hannah managed a weak smile.

"I promise."

Clara smoothed her skirt.

"Get some rest. The doctor said you should be fine to leave tomorrow. I'll be back to pick you up; you're staying with me for a few days until the dust settles." Clara scanned the room. "I'll ask Sheriff Reid to put one of his deputies on watch outside your room, just in case. Who knows what Jack Travis is really capable of."

Hannah's hand was up, palm out.

"No. No police. I'm not pressing charges anyway. The less attention we draw to this the better. And thanks for the offer but I think I'll be fine at my dad's house. My father's around most of the time anyway."

Clara nodded in agreement, leaned in for a hug, then spun around and left with an over-the-shoulder "No chances, remember."

She was out of the room before Hannah could say anything and she watched as the door sprang shut behind her employer.

Hannah smiled dimly, a warm feeling settling in her chest despite the trauma she'd gone through the night before. Because Clara Matthews was more than her employer. She was her mentor, a maternal figure who had genuine concern for her. A role Clara was happy to play since she never married or had children of her own. Though she incessantly warned Hannah not to let her ambition rob her of the opportunity to experience the joys she had missed out on, Hannah also knew that she would never rest until she got to the top and lived out her dreams in a swanky Manhattan apartment.

She closed her eyes and let out a sigh, her thoughts filled with a mixture of determination and trepidation.

There was no turning back now. Exposing Duncan Steele, owner of The Grande and tycoon billionaire of a chain of prestigious casinos, was precisely what was finally going to get her out of there.

# CHAPTER FIVE

Hours passed in a blur of medical checks and the soft hum of machinery. Nurses came and went, adjusting her IV, checking her vitals, and offering comforting smiles. Hannah appreciated their care, but her mind was elsewhere. She kept replaying the events of the night before, hoping to catch a glimpse of her rescuer in her fractured memories. Nothing. It was like trying to grasp at smoke.

By the time dusk settled outside her window, casting the room in a soft, orange glow, Hannah was restless. She knew Clara was right about one thing: she had to be more careful. But she couldn't let this small incident stop her. Weyport wasn't going to expose The Grande's secrets on its own.

A soft knock on the door interrupted her thoughts. A

young nurse, her blonde hair pulled back in a neat pony-tail, stepped in with a tray of food.

"Hi, Miss Jackson. How are you feeling?"

"I've been better," Hannah admitted, wincing as she shifted slightly. "Do you know when I can go home?"

The nurse offered a sympathetic smile.

"The doctor will be by soon to discuss that. But you should eat something in the meantime." She set the tray on the bedside table. "You need to keep your strength up."

Hannah nodded, but her appetite was nonexistent. She picked at the food, her mind still focused on the mystery person who saved her. Why had he helped her? Was he connected to The Grande somehow? Or was he just a passerby, an anonymous hero who happened to be in the right place at the right time?

Her thoughts were interrupted again, this time by the arrival of her doctor, a middle-aged man with kind eyes and a reassuring demeanor.

"Ms. Jackson, good to see you awake. How are you feeling?"

"Sore," Hannah admitted. "But I need to get back to work."

The doctor raised an eyebrow.

"You need to rest. You suffered a laceration and several bruised ribs. It's important that you take it easy for the next few days."

"I understand," she said, though her mind was already

racing ahead, planning her next move. "But I really need to get out of here."

He sighed, clearly used to dealing with stubborn patients.

"I'll discharge you tomorrow if everything looks good. But you must promise to take it easy."

"I promise," she lied, knowing full well she had no intention of resting. There was too much at stake.

THE FOLLOWING DAY, Hannah left the hospital with strict instructions to rest, a bottle of painkillers, and a warning look from the doctor. Clara had arranged a ride, a taxi driver with a handwritten note from her editor: "Don't make me regret this."

The ride home was a blur of pain and determination. She had told Clara she'd stay at her father's house, a little white lie Hannah told to appease her editor. Seeing her all battered and bruised would just fuel her father's argument and she wasn't about to give her father the satisfaction. The last thing she now needed was him telling her she would never make it as a New York reporter.

As soon as she was back in her small apartment, she sank into her couch, every muscle protesting the movement. The familiar surroundings brought her a strange comfort. Her laptop sat on the coffee table, beckoning her. She reached for it, ignoring the sharp protest from her ribs.

Opening it, she immediately began typing, her fingers flying across the keys as she documented every detail she could remember from the night before. The poker game, the alley, the attack. Her thoughts kept circling back to the mysterious rescuer. Who was he? What had he seen?

She pulled up the hospital's address on her phone and searched for possible nearby security cameras, hoping that one might have caught a glimpse of the person who saved her. It was a long shot, but it was all she had. After making a list of potential camera locations, she leaned back, exhaustion washing over her, the glow of her laptop screen casting shadows across her face. She was about to close her laptop when her phone buzzed, startling her. She picked it up, expecting a message from Clara or perhaps another concerned colleague from the *Weyport Herald*. Instead, it was an unknown number. Her heart raced as she read the message:

*"Meet me at the old lighthouse near Weyport Beach at midnight. I have information about The Grande. Come alone."*

HER BREATH CAUGHT in her throat. Could this be the Good Samaritan who saved her? Was this person reaching out to help her uncover the truth?

The message was terse, the timing urgent. Hannah's mind swirled with questions and possibilities. It could be a trap, but the promise of vital information about The Grande was too tempting to ignore.

She checked the clock. It was already 11 p.m. She had an hour to prepare.

After quickly changing into dark clothes, she grabbed a flashlight and tucked a small notebook into her jacket pocket. She debated calling Clara but decided against it. Clara would only try to talk her out of it. This was something she had to do on her own.

THE STREETS of Weyport were eerily quiet as she made her way to the beach. The moon hung low, casting a silver sheen over the water. The old lighthouse stood like a sentinel against the night sky, its once-bright light now dark and foreboding. When she reached the beach, the vast expanse of sand and sea stretched out before her, bathed in the pale light of the moon. The waves crashed relentlessly against the shore, adding to the eerie atmosphere. Her heart pounded in her chest as she checked her phone one last time. No new messages. She took a deep breath and moved closer to the lighthouse, her flashlight cutting through the darkness. The air was thick with the scent of salt and seaweed, mingling with the faint mustiness of the abandoned structure. She circled the base of the lighthouse, searching for any sign of her mysterious informant.

"Hello?" she called out softly, her voice barely audible above the roar of the ocean.

"Is anyone here?"

Silence.

The only response was the relentless crash of the waves. Hannah's nerves were on edge, every shadow seeming to move, every gust of wind sending shivers down her spine. She was about to turn back, her instincts screaming that something was wrong, when she heard a faint rustling behind her.

Spinning around, she aimed her flashlight into the darkness.

"Who's there?" she demanded, her voice trembling with a mix of fear and determination.

A figure emerged from the shadows, the person's face obscured by a hood.

"You came alone?" the figure asked, his voice low and distorted.

"Yes," Hannah replied, trying to keep her voice steady. "Who are you? What do you know about The Grande?"

The figure took a step closer with movements slow and deliberate.

"I know enough to help you," the person said. "But first, I need to know that I can trust you."

Hannah's mind raced. Could she trust a stranger in

the middle of the night at an abandoned lighthouse? She had no choice.

"Yes, you can. Tell me what you know," she said, keeping her flashlight trained on the shadowy figure whose face was entirely obscured by the hoodie he had closed up high over his nose.

"I have information about the people behind The Grande," the figure continued. "Names, numbers, illegal activities. But it's dangerous. They're watching me. They're watching everyone."

"So, it's true. The casino is a front," Hannah pressed.

Before the figure could answer, there was a sudden, sharp sound—a metallic clang against stone. The stranger whipped around and ran off into the darkness like a spooked deer.

Hannah barely had time to react before she felt a searing pain at the back of her head. Her vision blurred; the flashlight slipped from her grasp as she crumpled to the ground.

The last thing she saw before darkness claimed her was a tall, shadowy figure standing over her, his face hidden by the shadows. As unconsciousness pulled her under, one thought lingered in her mind: she had been so close to the truth, but now it seemed further away than ever.

# CHAPTER SIX

Hannah awoke to a pounding headache, her senses slowly returning as she tried to piece together what had happened. She was lying on cold, damp sand, the salty tang of the ocean filling her nostrils. The lighthouse loomed above her, its once protective structure now a silent witness to her attack.

Groaning, she pushed herself up, wincing as pain shot through her head. She touched the laceration to make sure the stitches hadn't opened up. Realizing the pain came from the back of her skull, she felt a tender lump where she'd been struck. Her flashlight lay a few feet away, its beam still faintly illuminating the sand.

She reached for it, the cold metal reassuring in her grasp. Her phone was still in her pocket, miraculously undamaged. She checked it—no new messages. The anonymous figure had vanished, leaving her with more questions than answers.

Hannah stood unsteadily, brushing the sand from her clothes. She scanned the area, looking for any clues her attacker might have left behind. But the beach was dark and empty; the only sound was the rhythmic crash of the waves. The sense of isolation was overwhelming.

She needed to get back to her apartment, regroup, and figure out her next move. The information her attacker had promised was tantalizing, but now she had to consider that someone else was aware of her investigation. Someone who wanted to stop her.

Back in her apartment, Hannah locked the door behind her, her fingers trembling as she slid the deadbolt into place. She leaned against the door, her mind racing. The pain in her head was a constant, throbbing reminder of how close she'd come to serious harm. Again.

She sank onto her couch, the adrenaline slowly draining from her body, leaving her exhausted. She couldn't afford to let fear take over. She was close to something big, and she couldn't back down now.

Hannah pulled out her notebook, flipping to the section where she'd detailed her investigation into The Grande. Names, dates, persons of interest—everything she'd uncovered so far was meticulously recorded. But it wasn't enough. She needed more.

Her thoughts returned to the mysterious message.

Who could have sent it? Was it someone from the poker tournament? One of the staff at The Grande? Or was it the Good Samaritan who had saved her in the alley?

Hannah's mind buzzed with unanswered questions as she stared at her notes. Her gut told her that the answer lay somewhere between the shadows of Weyport's underbelly and the opulent façade of The Grande. But how could she connect the dots without exposing herself to further danger?

SHE LET OUT A DEEP SIGH, her gaze shifting to the digital clock on her desk. 2:30 a.m. The night was creeping toward morning, yet sleep was far from her mind. Instead, she felt a renewed sense of determination.

Flipping through her notebook, Hannah reviewed the names of everyone she had encountered in her investigation. Among them, a few stood out: frequent players at the poker games, a couple of high rollers with questionable backgrounds, and staff at The Grande. One name, in particular seemed worth pursuing—Vincent Ward, a former dealer at The Grande who was abruptly fired six months ago under mysterious circumstances. Word around town was that Vincent had a falling out with the management, and since then, he had been living on the fringes of Weyport, laying low.

Hannah decided that she would interview Vincent

next. If anyone knew the inner workings of The Grande, it would be someone who had once been on the inside.

THE MORNING SUN cast a warm glow over Weyport, a stark contrast to the cold, damp darkness of the previous night. Hannah, despite her throbbing head and aching ribs, was up early, fueled by determination. She took a quick shower, dressed in a pair of jeans and a comfortable hoodie, and slipped out of her apartment, avoiding the silent warning at the back of her mind.

She had tracked down Vincent's address to the outskirts of town. The neighborhood was a stark contrast to the rest of Weyport—a series of rundown houses and abandoned buildings, a testament to the economic decline that had plagued parts of the community.

She parked her car a few blocks away from Vincent's last known address, a dilapidated apartment building with broken windows and peeling paint. Taking a deep breath, she approached the building, her senses on high alert. The quiet of the early morning was broken only by the occasional bark of a distant dog and the hum of a passing car.

Hannah reached Vincent's apartment, number 12B, on the second floor. She knocked on the door, her heart pounding. There was no response. She knocked again, louder this time. Still nothing. Frustration mingled with anxiety as she considered her next move. She couldn't afford to waste time.

Just as she was about to leave, she heard a shuffling from inside. She knocked one more time, harder.

"Who is it?" a gruff voice called from within.

"Vincent? It's Hannah Jackson. I'm a journalist with the *Weyport Herald*. I need to talk to you about The Grande. It's urgent."

There was a long pause. Hannah held her breath, hoping he wouldn't dismiss her outright.

The door creaked open a few inches, and a pair of weary eyes peered out at her. Vincent looked disheveled, his once sharp features now shadowed by days of stubble and dark circles under his eyes.

"What do you want?" he asked, his voice tinged with suspicion.

"I need your help," Hannah said earnestly. "I'm investigating The Grande. I believe you have information that could be crucial to my story. Please, it's important."

Vincent's eyes narrowed.

"Why should I trust you? I don't want any more trouble."

"I understand," Hannah replied, her tone softening. "But I'm trying to expose the truth. I was attacked a couple of nights ago because I'm getting too close. Someone saved me, and I'm hoping you might know who it was or why he did. Please, I just need a few minutes."

Vincent hesitated, then opened the door wider.

"All right, come in. But make it quick."

Hannah stepped inside, the musty smell of the apartment hitting her as she entered. The place was sparsely furnished, with only a worn-out couch, a small table, and a few scattered belongings. Vincent motioned for her to sit on the couch, and she did so, carefully.

"Thank you," she said, her gratitude genuine.

Vincent sat opposite her, his expression guarded.

"What do you want to know?"

"Everything you can tell me about The Grande," Hannah began, "especially about Duncan Steele and Jack Travis. What happened between you and them?"

Vincent sighed, running a hand through his messy hair.

"Off the record. If they know I'm talking to the press I'm as good as dead."

"You have my word."

He paused then continued.

"The Grande is a front for something much bigger. I'm not exactly sure what but my guess would be money laundering, illegal gambling rings, you name it. I found out by accident, stumbled on some documents I wasn't supposed to see. I got caught and they fired me. The end."

"Why didn't you go to the authorities?" Hannah asked.

Vincent let out a bitter laugh.

"You think the cops in this county aren't on their

payroll? They own this place, Hannah. Steele's got everyone in his pocket."

Hannah nodded, silently wondering if she'd gauged Sheriff Reid wrongly and if it was possible that he was capable of being bribed. She dismissed the thought, choosing to believe the best of him.

"Do you know who might have saved me the other night? Someone left me at the hospital after I was attacked in the alley behind the Turkish barbershop on Fifth Street."

Vincent's eyes darkened.

"I heard about what happened. Word travels fast in the underground. I have an idea, but I can't be sure. There's a guy, used to be close to Steele, but they had a falling out. Goes by the name of Lucas. He's been trying to bring Steele down ever since. It's possible he's the one who helped you."

Hannah's pulse quickened.

"Do you know where I can find him?"

"He's a ghost," Vincent said with a shrug. "Moves around a lot, but I've heard he frequents a bar on the east side of town. The Black Cat. If you're lucky, you might catch him there."

Hannah jotted the name of the bar in her notebook.

"Thank you, Vincent. This could be the break I need."

"Be careful, Hannah," Vincent warned. "Steele and Travis are dangerous men. They won't think twice about silencing anyone who gets in their way."

"I will," she promised. "And thank you again. You've been a great help."

AS HANNAH LEFT Vincent's apartment, her mind was already racing with the next steps. She had a new lead—Lucas—and was one step closer to busting open the biggest story of her career.

# CHAPTER SEVEN

The Black Cat was a dimly lit, nondescript bar tucked away in a back alley on the east side of Weyport. Hannah arrived just after dusk. The neon sign flickered ominously in the twilight. The bar had a reputation for being a hangout for the town's more dubious characters, but she had no choice. If Lucas was her only link to the truth, she had to take the risk.

She pushed open the heavy wooden door and stepped inside. The bar was crowded, filled with the hum of low conversations and the clink of glasses. The smell of alcohol and cigarette smoke hung thick in the air. Hannah scanned the room, looking for anyone who might match Vincent's description of Lucas.

She made her way to the bar and ordered a drink, keeping her eyes peeled for any sign of her elusive target. After a few minutes, she spotted a man sitting alone in a corner booth, his face partially obscured by the hood of his jacket. Something about his demeanor suggested he was trying to avoid attention.

Gathering her courage, Hannah approached the booth.

"Lucas?" she asked softly.

The man looked up, his sharp eyes assessing her.

"Who's asking?"

"Hannah Jackson," she replied. "I'm a journalist. I'm investigating the rumors about The Grande."

Lucas's expression didn't change, but his eyes flickered with emotion.

"What makes you think I can help?" he asked, gesturing to the seat opposite him.

Hannah slid into the booth, her heart pounding.

"A source who used to work at The Grande said you might know something."

He grunted.

"Also, I think you were the one who rescued me in the alley the other night. Thank you. I don't know what would have happened if you hadn't shown up."

There was no reaction in his eyes when Hannah said it. Instead, his voice was blunt when he eventually spoke.

"Why are you chasing after Steele and Travis? Do you have a death wish or something?"

"I'm a journalist," Hannah replied. "I want to expose the truth. The people of Weyport deserve to know what's really going on at The Grande. And I need your help. As I understand it, you need mine too."

Lucas studied her for a moment.

"What gives you that idea?"

"You saved me for a reason, didn't you? In my experience that means you have a motive, perhaps even a score to settle. So, the way I see it, we can help each other. Bust this thing wide open and give Steele and Travis what they deserve - time behind bars."

Lucas dropped his gaze to the beer in his hand before he looked up then nodded.

"Even if I do decide to help you, it will be on my terms. These men are ruthless. They won't hesitate to kill to protect their secrets."

Hannah's heart leaped with excitement.

"I understand," she said, her voice steady. "But I can't walk away now. I'm too close. Can you tell me what you know?"

Lucas leaned back in his seat. After a long pause, he answered.

"You keep me out of it, got it?"

She nodded. "I never reveal my sources. You can trust me."

Lucas drained what was left of his beer and leaned in over the table. "Steele is running a massive money laundering operation through The Grande. In fact, every casino he owns is part of his scheme. He's got connections in every industry, including law enforcement and local government. Jack Travis is his enforcer, the one who deals with anyone who gets too close to the truth. He keeps a close eye on the players and vets them without them even knowing." He scoffed and sat back in his seat. "Even the backstreet poker games are rigged."

Hannah listened intently, taking mental notes. That's how Jack must have found out who she was.

"So, these poker tournaments are part of the scam? A way to onboard high rollers they can swindle out of money."

"In a manner of speaking," Lucas confirmed. "The high-stakes games are a front for moving large sums of money without drawing attention. They rig the games to ensure their people win and lose strategically, keeping the money flowing in the right direction."

"And keep people like me at bay."

He nodded.

Hannah felt a surge of vindication. She had suspected as much, but having it confirmed was a breakthrough. "Do you have any proof? Documents, recordings, anything?"

Lucas shook his head.

"I've been trying to get my hands on solid evidence for years, but it's been tough. I don't have deep enough pockets to pay for it either. I fell victim to his swindling myself." His voice was tinged with anger when he said it.

"I see. What else can you tell me?"

Lucas scratched the back of his hand.

"Steele keeps everything well-hidden. Believe me, I've tried. At least while I still had access to the building."

"So, you worked at The Grande?"

"I guess you could say that."

Lucas shifted in his seat.

"You were close once, correct?" Hannah knew she was pushing him too hard, but she couldn't hold back now.

"I think we're done here, Miss Jackson." He started sliding out of the booth.

"No stop, I'm sorry. I get it. I overstepped the line. Just tell me where I might find the necessary documents to back up these claims and you never have to see me again." Her voice was urgent, her breath caught in her throat as she watched Lucas perch on the edge of the booth.

After a long pause he slipped back into the booth, his eyes fixed on hers.

"He keeps everything in an encrypted file on his computer. It's impossible to crack."

Hannah's shoulders dropped with disappointment.

"There has to be another way, a paper trail, anything." Her voice was desperate.

Lucas's eyes narrowed.

"I know someone who might be able to help. He's expensive though. He charges the kind of money I don't have, and since you're a small-town reporter, I'm guessing will be out of your range as well."

Hannah leaned in, her heart rate ticking up with hope. "Who?"

Her enthusiasm had caught Lucas by surprise, and he fell silent.

"Who Lucas? Please tell me."

His palms turned upward as he dropped his head into a slight nod.

"There's a hacker who goes by the name of Shadow. If anyone can get into Steele's files, it's him."

"Where can I find this Shadow guy?" Hannah asked, eager for the next lead.

Lucas hesitated.

"He's not easy to find. Hence his name." The corner of his mouth curled into a smile. "He moves around a lot, just like me. But I've heard he works out of an old warehouse near the docks somewhere. If you're serious about this, then he's your best bet."

Hannah nodded, determination etched on her face.

"Thank you, Lucas. I'll find him."

"Be careful," Lucas warned again. "You're playing a dangerous game."

"I know," Hannah said, standing up. "But I'm not backing down."

As she left The Black Cat, Hannah felt a renewed sense of purpose. With a lead on a hacker who could help her get the evidence she needed, she knew the path forward was fraught with danger, but she was more resolved than ever to see this through.

# CHAPTER EIGHT

The warehouse district near the docks was a labyrinth of abandoned buildings and rusting shipping containers. Hannah arrived late in the evening, the air thick with the smell of saltwater and diesel. She navigated the maze of narrow streets and alleys, her footsteps echoing off the walls.

Minutes stretched into hours as she wound her way between the warehouses, nearly all of them unoccupied and locked. When her throbbing headache nearly made her give up the search, Hannah finally found the exception. It stood at the end of a desolate row, its windows boarded up and the metal door hanging ajar. She approached cautiously, peering inside. The interior was dark, the only light coming from a few flickering bulbs strung haphazardly across the ceiling.

"Shadow?" she called out, her voice barely above a whisper.

For a moment, there was no response. Then, a figure emerged from the shadows, a young man with a scruffy beard and a laptop under his arm.

"Who are you?" he asked, his tone wary.

"Hannah Jackson. I'm a journalist. Lucas sent me. I need your help."

Shadow's eyes narrowed. "What kind of help?"

"I need to get into Duncan Steele's files," Hannah explained. "I need proof of his illegal activities."

Shadow studied her for a moment. "I don't trust reporters," he said, then turned to leave.

"No, wait! I can pay you."

He stopped mid-turn.

"How do I know you are who you say you are and that this isn't a trap?"

She pointed to his laptop.

"Look me up. *Weyport Herald.* My editor is Clara Matthews."

"Anyone can put up a fake website."

She paused for a moment, then reached inside her purse and pulled out her driver's license.

"Here, see?" She held it out toward him.

"Why do you need access to his files?"

"I suspect he's laundering money. I need evidence."

Shadow handed back her license, studied her for a few seconds more, then nodded.

"It's going to cost you."

"I can pay. How much?"

"Ten thousand dollars upfront, another ten if I get you what you want."

"Deal!"

Her hand disappeared back inside her purse and she pulled out two poker chips.

"Will these do?"

She handed him one and he scrutinized it to make sure it wasn't fake.

"It might as well have been crypto," he said and buried it in his pocket, a slight twinkle in his eye.

"All right. Follow me."

Hannah's heart nearly pounded out of her chest. This was it! The break in her investigation she'd been waiting for. If Shadow's efforts were successful, she'd have all the proof she needed to crack this story wide open. Her face flushed with joy as she trailed behind.

Shadow led her deeper into the warehouse to a makeshift workstation cluttered with monitors and computer equipment. He sat down and began typing furiously, his fingers a blur on the keyboard, his eyes darting back and forth between the coded letters on his screen.

"This won't be easy," he said after a short while, his eyes never leaving the screen. "Steele's got some serious security on his systems."

"So I've heard. I also understand you're the best in the business," Hannah replied. "I cannot leave here without this, Shadow. I need this. It's the only way to bring him down."

Shadow continued working, the hum of the computers filling the silence. For the better part of several hours, Hannah watched, her nerves on edge. Finally, Shadow leaned back, a triumphant smile on his face.

"I'm in," he said.

"You're in? Really?" Hannah exclaimed, barely able to contain her excitement.

"Give me a few more minutes to download everything."

Hannah's heart raced with anticipation. This was it— the breakthrough she needed. Nearly a year's worth of work that was finally beginning to pay off. She watched as Shadow transferred files onto a flash drive, her mind already racing with how she would use the evidence to expose Steele and Travis.

But as Shadow handed her the flash drive, the sound of footsteps echoed through the warehouse. Someone was coming, and judging from Shadow's stiff spine, it wasn't anyone he was expecting. Hannah's blood ran cold.

"Hide," Shadow hissed, shoving her toward a stack of crates. "Quickly!"

Hannah ducked behind the crates, clutching the flash drive tightly. The footsteps grew louder, accompanied by the low murmur of voices. She peered through a gap in the crates, her heart pounding in her throat.

A group of men had entered the warehouse, led by none other than Jack Travis.

Her mind flooded with questions. How did he know she was there? Was she being followed? Was she careless and had led them straight to the warehouse? Her heart sank into her stomach. She watched as his cold eyes scanned the room, landing on Shadow.

"Where is she?" Travis demanded as two of his men yanked Shadow from his hiding place and deposited him at their employer's feet.

"I don't know what you're talking about," Shadow replied, his voice steady.

Travis's eyes narrowed.

"Don't play games with me. We know she's here."

"Who? I'm here alone," Shadow lied.

A large muscle-bound man whipped the back of his hand across Shadow's face.

Shadow groaned but looked Travis dead in the eyes. Moments later the muscled man moved to deliver another punch, except this time Shadow fought back, blocking the man's large forearm before his fist made contact with his face. Shadow seized the moment and drove his fist into the man's ear. His attempt at fighting back had little to no effect and only left the man livid.

He yanked Shadow up on his feet.

Shadow clutched at the man's strong arms before his large forehead slammed into Shadow's nose.

"Enough! Spread out and find her!" Travis yelled.

Panic surged through Hannah as the men began searching the warehouse. She pressed herself against the crates, her mind racing. She couldn't let them find her. Not now, not when she was so close.

As the men drew nearer, Hannah's hand brushed against something cold and metal. A small, rusted pipe lay hidden behind the crates. She picked it up, her grip tightening. If they found her, she would have to fight.

The search drew closer, the sound of footsteps and rustling growing louder. Hannah held her breath, her heart hammering in her chest. She was ready to defend herself, no matter the cost.

Suddenly, a shout rang out.

"Over here!"

Hannah's heart stopped. She squeezed her eyes shut. One of Travis's men had spotted her.

*Don't be a coward, Hannah! Do it!*

She sprang to her feet, brandishing the pipe.

"Stay back!" she warned, her voice trembling.

The men closed in, but before they could reach her, a gunshot rang out. Hannah froze, her eyes wide with horror as she saw Shadow collapse to the ground, a dark stain spreading across his chest.

"No!" she screamed, rushing toward him.

Travis grabbed her from behind, his grip like a vice.

"You're coming with us," he snarled.

"And this time there's no one to save you."

Hannah struggled, but it was no use. The last thing she saw was Shadow's lifeless body as Travis's men dragged her out of the warehouse.

# CHAPTER NINE

Angus was poring over a cold case file on his desk when Tammy popped her head around his office door.

"Got a moment, Sheriff?"

"Of course. What's up?"

"I've got Clara Matthews from the *Weyport Herald* on the line. She just filed a missing person's report on Hannah Jackson."

"Missing? Did she give any more details? I mean, she's a reporter. Don't reporters go off on leads all the time?"

"Probably, except she says Hannah hasn't been seen or heard from in a few days. She was supposed to come into work this morning but never did. According to Miss Matthews, it's not like her. Apparently, Hannah's never been late for work. Ever. Nor has she been absent without at least a text message. She also said Hannah was brutally attacked a few nights ago and that she's working on a big story for the paper."

"What kind of story?"

"She didn't want to divulge. Said it's too dangerous."

Angus leaned back in his chair and closed the folder on his desk. His mind began to churn through the possibilities. This was clearly no ordinary disappearance.

"Thanks, Tammy. You can put her call through, please."

Tammy nodded and scurried back to her desk. Moments later, the phone on Angus's desk rang.

"Clara?" he answered. "What's this about Hannah being missing?"

"Sheriff, I'm really worried," Clara's voice trembled slightly. "Hannah's been working on a story about The Grande Casino. She's convinced there's something sinister going on and just wouldn't let it go. If you ask me her determination to gain her father's respect is clouding her judgement but you know Hannah. Once she has her mind made up there's no changing it. So, I let her run with the rumors about the machines being rigged but then she was attacked last week, and now she's vanished."

"Attacked how? I don't recall seeing the report." Angus rifled through the papers on his desk.

"She didn't want to press charges. It would have jeopardized the investigation."

"I see. Tell me everything you know about her investigation," Angus demanded, his voice taking on a sterner edge. "And don't leave anything out."

Clara sighed, the sound of papers shuffling faintly audible through the line. "Hannah believes The Grande is involved in money laundering and illegal gambling. It's a crazy idea, I know, but I've been in this business long enough to know that where there's a rumor, there's a story. And Hannah...well, as you know, she's a stubborn little one who has far too much ambition for a small town like Weyport. Anyway, I let her run with the investigation, just in the event these rumors ring true. She's been at it nearly a year now, working her way through backstreet poker games trying to gather evidence. Incognito, of course. I don't have the full picture yet, there are still a lot of missing links and nothing to substantiate anything note-worthy, but I think that's why she was assaulted the other night while at one of these games. They discovered her true identity and somehow figured out she was a reporter. Anyway, like I said, she didn't want to press charges and decided to chase down another lead. Last time we spoke, she mentioned meeting someone who knew a guy who could help her get the proof she needed to bust this story wide open. That was nearly two days ago. I haven't heard from her since."

Angus felt a chill run down his spine. The Grande had been on his radar for years, but he'd never been able to get enough evidence to open any kind of investigation. And it was just the kind of story Hannah would chase. If indeed her disappearance was connected to her investigation, that meant she was in real danger since he suspected that there was a lot more brewing beyond the casino walls.

"Where was she attacked, and does she know who it was?"

Clara grew silent.

"Clara?"

"Yes, sorry, I'm here. In the back alley behind the Turkish barbershop on Fifth."

"Why was she there? I mean, it's not the sort of place a woman hangs out after dark."

Clara hesitated.

"Clara, what aren't you telling me? If you want me to find Hannah, you need to tell me everything."

Clara sighed.

"It's where the illegal poker games take place, in the back of the barbershop."

Angus rubbed one hand across his brows, careful not to divulge how he truly felt about Hannah's foolish methods to get a story.

"Did she know who attacked her?"

"It was dark, Sheriff. Someone interrupted them, stopped them from kidnapping her and dropped her off at the hospital. A Good Samaritan who took every precaution not to have his identity known. That's who she went after, the other lead I said she decided to follow."

Angus could hear the panic escalating in Clara's voice.

"And you say she was meeting someone. Do you have

any idea who she was meeting or where she might have gone?"

"No," Clara replied, frustration evident in her tone. "She's always been very protective of her sources. I just assumed she might have found out who her secret Samaritan was."

"I'll look into this. There has to be a surveillance camera somewhere that caught the person entering the hospital."

"There isn't, I've already checked with the hospital. It's like he knew which angles to avoid."

"I see. I'm assuming it goes without saying that you've already called her mobile and checked if she was home," Angus continued.

"Her phone goes to voicemail, and I don't have a key to her apartment. Not that she would be there anyway. I told her to stay at her father's and as far as I'm aware, that's where she was staying."

"And did she? Did you check with her father?"

"I thought of it, but I didn't want to alarm him. We don't exactly see eye to eye. He's accused me of fueling Hannah's ambition, giving her false hope and all. I reckon he just hates all women. Period."

"Why is that?"

Clara snickered.

"Because he doesn't hold back on how little he thinks of women. Ever since his wife left him to chase after some job offer in LA, he's been very vocal about how a woman should be home serving her husband and raising kids instead of chasing after a corporate career because she isn't good enough to succeed. As far as he's concerned, women aren't smart enough to do a man's job."

"Sounds like something my father said to my mother once," Angus said ruefully and then he continued. "Okay, sit tight and stay close to the phone in case she calls. If she or anyone else calls, you let us know right away. Until proven otherwise, we have to assume she might have been kidnapped. I'll send you my cell number."

Angus's fingers were already busy on his cellphone.

"Please, Sheriff, you know she's like a daughter to me. Find her," Clara's voice broke, and Angus could feel her desperation.

"I promise, Clara. We'll do everything we can to find her."

After hanging up, Angus popped his head out of his office door and called to Miguel Garcia, who was sitting at his desk.

"Miguel, come with me. We have a missing person case—Hannah Jackson. She's been investigating The Grande Casino and might be in serious trouble."

"Yes, Sheriff. Right behind you."

ANGUS GRABBED his jacket and keys, his mind already racing through the next steps. If Hannah's disappearance was connected to her investigation, she was in over her head. His own investigations had taught him that Duncan Steele was not to be underestimated. He had friends in very high places, and not all of them were above board. And if there was a chance, even a slim one, that Duncan Steele was behind Hannah's disappearance, time was of the essence. Angus had had his fair share of dealings with casino owners back in Las Vegas. They were slick and they were always dirty.

Finding Hannah was crucial. Finding her alive was his biggest concern.

# CHAPTER TEN

ngus and Miguel drove in silence, the weight of the situation pressing down on them. The streets of Weyport passed by in a blur as Angus reviewed what he knew about The Grande Casino. Over the years, whispers of its illicit activities had circulated, but no one had been able to pin anything solid on Duncan Steele. As far as the world was concerned, he was a saint. Hannah's investigation might have been the closest anyone had come to uncovering the truth.

The tension in the truck was palpable as they approached Hannah Jackson's apartment building and Angus's mind raced with thoughts of what they might find, praying it wouldn't be her body. They parked the truck and stepped into the cool evening air, the crunch of gravel under their boots the only sound breaking the silence.

The apartment building was a modest, three-story structure of faded brick with ivy creeping up the walls. Angus led the way up the front steps, his flashlight cutting through the dim light as Miguel reached for the doorbell to her apartment. He pressed it and listened intently, but there was no response. After a moment, Angus turned to Miguel.

"Try the superintendent. We need access to her apartment. If she's not inside, she might have left something that can give us a lead," Angus said, his voice low but firm, conveying the urgency of the situation.

The apartment manager was quick to let them in and ushered them up the narrow staircase to the second floor. The hallway was dimly lit, the flickering bulbs casting an eerie glow on the worn carpet. They reached Hannah's apartment, number 204, where he knocked then unlocked the door.

"I'll leave you to it, Sheriff," he said. "If you need anything else, you know where to find me."

Angus thanked him and turned his attention to Hannah's apartment.

"Hannah? It's Sheriff Reid. Can we talk?" he called out, but the only response was the distant hum of a television from another apartment.

They pushed the door open and stepped inside, their flashlights sweeping the room. The apartment was neat yet showed signs of recent activity—papers were strewn across the coffee table, and a laptop was left open on the couch.

"She left in a hurry," Miguel observed, picking up a stack of handwritten notes and flipping through them.

Angus nodded, his eyes scanning the room for any clues.

"Let's see what we can find. Check the laptop, and I'll look through these notes."

Miguel moved to the couch and began examining the laptop, his fingers flying over the keys. Angus focused on the notepad on the coffee table, filled with scribbled addresses and times. His brow furrowed as he flipped through the pages, each entry providing a glimpse into Hannah's relentless pursuit of a story.

"This might be something," Angus said, holding up the notepad. "Looks like she was tracking someone named Vincent."

Angus felt a surge of hope, knowing that every second counted.

"Vincent. It's a start. There's an address here. Maybe he knows something."

Before leaving, Angus took one last look around the apartment. Hannah's determination and bravery were evident in the scattered clues she had left behind. He silently promised to find her and bring her back safely.

"Let's go," Angus said, his voice steady with resolve.

THE ADDRESS LED them to a rundown apartment building on the other side of town. The area was a stark contrast to the more well-kept parts of Weyport, with cracked sidewalks and overgrown weeds adding to the sense of neglect. Angus and Miguel approached cautiously, their senses on high alert. They knocked on the door of the specified apartment.

"Weyport Sheriff's Department," Angus called out. "We need to ask you a few questions."

There was a shuffling sound inside, and the door creaked open. A disheveled young man with weary eyes peered out at them.

"Are you Vincent Ward?" Angus asked.

"Yes. What's this about?" Vincent replied, his voice edged with suspicion.

"We're looking for Hannah Jackson. She's gone missing, and we believe you might have information that could help us find her."

Vincent's eyes widened with recognition and fear.

"Come in, quickly."

Inside, the apartment was sparse, with papers and electronics scattered around. Vincent motioned for them to sit.

"Look, I don't know where she is," Vincent began, his voice trembling. "Yes, she was here a few days ago. Asked me all sorts of questions about when I worked at The Grande and why I got fired. Said it was for a story she was working on. That's it, that's all I know."

Vincent jumped up and started pacing the room as he nervously chewed on the nail of his little finger.

"You worked at the casino and got fired," Angus repeated, his voice pitching into a question.

"Yes, a while ago, but I've moved on. I don't want any trouble."

Angus and Miguel exchanged a glance, a nonverbal acknowledgement of Vincent's nervous behavior.

"Why were you fired?" Miguel asked.

Vincent grunted, his hand sweeping back and forth through his already messy hair.

"I told you, I don't want any trouble. I didn't tell her anything, I swear. She was here; I told her what she needed to know and then she left. That's it."

"Then you have nothing to worry about, Vincent. Just answer the question. Why were you fired?"

Vincent's eyes were big, the white of his eyes in stark contrast with the dark circles below.

"I found some documents I wasn't supposed to find, got caught looking at them, and got fired. That's it, man. I swear I didn't do anything, and I don't know where this chick is either. I just wanna move on with my life. Why can't you people leave me alone?"

A frown burrowed above Angus's eyes.

"What do you mean, Vincent? Which people?" Angus prodded.

Vincent slumped onto the couch.

"Look, if you're in Duncan Steele's pocket you can tell him I've kept my word."

Surprise flashed across Miguel's face.

"So that's what's got you so nervous. You think we're crooked cops on Duncan Steele's payroll."

Vincent looked up from where he sat with his head in his hands.

"You're not?"

"Nope, we're as honest as they come," Angus said. "So, do you want to start over now and tell us exactly what you said to Miss Jackson, please so we can find her before it's too late?"

Vincent was on his feet again, his hands on his hips, his head thrown back as he let go of the tension that haunted him only a few moments before.

"I'm sorry for doubting you, Sheriff. These people are not to be messed with, you know. I needed to be sure that's all."

He puffed out his cheeks before he sat back down on the couch.

"She came here wanting to know if I knew who might have saved her from Travis's guys the other night."

"Travis?" Miguel queried.

"Yes, Jack Travis. He's Duncan Steele's right hand man."

"So, he attacked her?" Angus asked.

"Who else? Word on the street is she played in one of his poker games and when he found out that she was a reporter, he did what he always does for Steele - makes problems disappear before they come back to bite him in the rear."

"And? Do you know who helped her get away?" Miguel asked.

Vincent nodded as he lit a cigarette.

"There's this guy who used to be close to Steele, best friends, started the casino together if I remember the story correctly. But they had a falling out. No one knows why but he's been trying to bring Steele down ever since. I told her it might have been him. Goes by the name of Lucas."

Vincent puffed out tiny ringlets of smoke.

"And where might we find this Lucas guy?" Angus asked.

Vincent laughed.

"You won't. I told her the same thing. He's a ghost, stays out of sight. If he wants to be seen, he'll find you. Especially if there are cops sniffing around."

"So, you're saying you have no idea where he might be," Miguel said.

"No, I'm saying you won't find him."

"Try me," Angus challenged, his eyes narrowing with warning.

"Fine, but don't come crying to me if he sucks up your time." He paused then told them about the The Black Cat bar on the east side of town.

"Is this where you sent Miss Jackson?" Angus asked to which Vincent nodded.

Feelings of frustration and determination filled Angus as he and Miguel thanked Vincent and left.

# CHAPTER ELEVEN

As they left Vincent's apartment, Angus's mind raced. The deeper they dug, the more dangerous the situation became and the less everything made sense. He'd always known that Duncan Steele was a man of influence but now knowing just how deep that influence ran had him feeling more than unsettled. If what Vincent said held truth and Hannah poked the hornet's nest in search of a story, she could be in serious danger.

He took a deep breath to steady his nerves when they got to his truck.

"Think he's telling the truth, Sheriff?" Miguel cut into his thoughts.

"Which part?"

"The crooked cops part."

"I'd like to believe he's lying, Miguel, but the truth of the matter is that money talks. I saw it back in Vegas all the time. Judges were paid off to look the other way; cops, even confidential informants were poached and paid off. Money buys loyalty. It's the root of all evil."

"Well, not me, Sheriff. I can't be bought."

Angus gestured his gratitude with a quick nod.

"Let's head to The Black Cat," he suggested as they got into the truck. "If there's a chance this Lucas guy was the last one to see Hannah, we should take it. Time is crucial."


THEY ARRIVED at The Black Cat just after dusk, the neon sign flickering ominously in the twilight. Angus knew the dubious nature of the bar's patrons well, but this time he wasn't there to break up a drunken fight. Lucas was their only link to finding Hannah, and if it meant getting answers in a place like this, Angus was prepared to do whatever it took.

Angus and Miguel pushed open the heavy, wooden door and stepped inside. The bar was crowded, filled with the hum of low conversations and the clink of glasses. The smell of alcohol and cigarette smoke hung thick in the air. They made their way to the bar, keeping their eyes peeled for any sign of their so-called elusive target.

"We're looking for someone named Lucas," Angus said quietly to the barman.

The barman's expression didn't change, but his eyes flickered with something unreadable.

"Don't know anyone by that name," he replied gruffly.

Angus glanced around the room, noticing the tight-lipped demeanor of the patrons.

"We're just trying to find a woman," he pressed. "Any information would be helpful."

"No one here by that name," the barman repeated, turning his back on them.

Miguel leaned closer to Angus.

"They're not going to talk. They're protecting the guy."

Angus scanned the room again, his eyes landing on a lone figure in a corner booth, partially obscured by the shadows. The man was watching them intently, his hood pulled low over his face. Something about his demeanor suggested he was the one they were looking for.

"Let's try over there," Angus said, nodding toward the corner booth.

As they approached, the man looked up, his sharp eyes assessing them.

"What do you want?" he asked, his voice low and guarded.

"Are you Lucas?" Angus asked.

"Depends on why you're asking," the man replied.

"I'm Sheriff Reid, and this is my deputy, Miguel. We're looking for Hannah Jackson. We believe you might have recently been in contact with her."

The man's face was blank as he stared back at Angus.

"I have no idea what you're talking about, Sheriff. I'm not exactly the kind of guy women like to be with."

The hooded man's attention turned back to the game of solitaire he was playing on the table in front of him.

"Oh, I don't know, Lucas," Angus ventured. "I think you're precisely the kind of guy Miss Jackson would interview. And we happen to know that she was sent here to see you. We also know that she's not been seen since so it looks to me like you'd better start telling us about your meeting. We can do it here, in front of everyone in a calm and peaceful manner, or you can take a ride down to the station with us. Your choice. Which will it be?"

The guy scooped up his playing cards, tapping them on the table to tidy up the deck before he looked up at Angus.

"Like I said, Sheriff, I haven't seen this woman and I have no idea who Lucas is either." His hand disappeared inside his back pocket. Moments later he tossed his driver's license on the table in front of him. "See for yourself."

Angus scooped up the card, his eyes never leaving the man's face until he read the name on the card. Ross Mead. He glanced between the man's face and the photo on the card.

"Now do you believe me? You've got the wrong guy, Sheriff," the man said as he skillfully shuffled the pack of cards.

Frustration tugged at the back of Angus's mind as he tossed the man's driver's license onto the table.

"Do you know where we might find Lucas?"

Ross Mead dealt the cards on the table in front of him.

"Like I said, Sheriff, I have no idea who or where this guy is. Now if there's nothing else you'd like to harass me with, I'd like to get back to my game, please."

Angus paused briefly, his emotions threatening to explode with anger at the man's obvious deceit.

"Sorry to have bothered you, Mr. Mead. Enjoy your evening," he said before he and Miguel turned and left the bar.

When they were outside, standing in front of his truck, Angus couldn't hide his frustration any longer.

"Something's not adding up here, Miguel. I can feel it. Either that guy is lying and he *is* Lucas, or he knows something."

Miguel was already on the passenger side of the vehicle.

"I agree. This guy knows something, but you saw his identification card yourself. He's clearly not this Lucas guy Vincent mentioned. For all we know Vincent sent us on a wild goose chase. Who knows? I reckon we pay the Turkish barber a visit and circle back to this guy after I run a check on him."

Angus nodded in agreement and slipped behind the wheel of his truck, his knuckles white as he gripped the steering wheel.

"Get onto it right away, Miguel. I want to know everything there is to know about Ross Mead. I know a liar when I see one and every bone in my body tells me he knows a lot more than he's letting on."

"We'll find Hannah, Sheriff. She's as feisty as they come. A fighter. From what I've heard, she's not one to back down from a story. Perhaps she realized she's in danger and she's hiding out somewhere."

Angus pushed his foot down harder on the pedal.

"I hope you're right, Miguel, because I have an uneasy feeling about this case I just cannot seem to shake."

# CHAPTER TWELVE

They arrived at the Turkish barbershop on Fifth Street fifteen minutes later. The alley behind the shop was deserted, littered with debris and cast in the shadows of the surrounding buildings. Angus and Miguel stepped out of the truck, their breath visible in the cool evening air.

"This is where Clara said Hannah was attacked," Angus said, scanning the area. "Let's look around and see if we can find anything that might get us closer to finding out what happened that night."

They moved carefully through the alley, examining the ground for any signs of a struggle. Angus's flashlight beam swept across the pavement, illuminating discarded items and patches of darkness.

"Sheriff, over here," Miguel called out, pointing to a

small pool of dried blood near the wall. "Looks like this might have been where she was attacked."

Angus crouched down, his stomach twisting at the sight.

He beamed his flashlight over the spot, then across the surrounding areas. Something caught his eye. Something shiny.

He moved closer, shining the flashlight directly onto the tiny, shimmering object.

"It looks like it's part of an earring. One of those with the single diamonds," Miguel pointed out. "And it's covered in blood," he added.

Angus slipped on a black latex glove and transferred it into an evidence bag.

"Think it's Hannah's?" Miguel asked.

"It's possible. Get forensics here ASAP and have them block off the alley. Hannah might not have wanted to report her assault, but until we know more, we have to treat this as a possible crime scene. Or, at the very least, a run-up to her disappearance. I need evidence that Jack Travis assaulted her so I can bring him in for questioning."

He stood and scanned the rest of the area.

"Do you think he tried to finish the job?" Miguel said as he called in the request to the forensics team.

"If he did, let's hope he failed a second time."

When Miguel ended his call, he turned his attention back to the shadowy corners of the alley.

"Maybe the Good Samaritan left something behind

too," Miguel suggested. "If we're lucky and he left his prints or DNA behind, we might have a better chance at tracking him down. Whoever it was, he is now a key witness to her assault."

Angus turned his gaze toward the barbershop's door in search of surveillance cameras, but there were none.

"Well, we're out of luck with getting our hands on any CCTV footage. There's not a single camera in this alley. Almost as if they were intentionally creating a blind spot."

Frustration gnawed at Angus. He glanced around, feeling the cold wind bite at his skin.

"I think it's time we talk to the owner of the barber-shop," Angus decided. "If he is allowing Travis to illegally run a gambling ring from the back of his shop, chances are he won't talk, but it's worth a shot until I catch the guy in the act."

He covered the short distance to the barbershop's back door and rapped on it loudly. When no one answered, Angus glanced at his watch.

"Cordon off the alley, Miguel, and wait for forensics. I'm going around to the front."

Angus rounded the corner and approached the front door of the Turkish barbershop. The warm glow of the shop's interior lights spilled out onto the sidewalk, a stark contrast to the cold, dark alley. He pushed open the door, the bell above it chiming softly as he stepped inside.

The owner, a burly man with graying hair and a thick mustache, was just finishing with one of his clients. The smell of shaving cream and aftershave filled the air. The owner looked up as Angus entered, his eyes narrowing slightly.

"Evening, Sheriff. What brings you here this late in the day?" the barber asked, his voice gruff but polite.

"Good evening," Angus replied, his tone serious. "I need to ask you a few questions about an incident that happened in the alley behind your shop a few nights ago. A young woman was attacked."

The barber's eyes stretched open.

"Attacked? Behind my shop?"

Angus answered with a nod as the barber finished trimming his client's hair and removed the cape with a practiced flourish.

"I wasn't aware. Must have happened after I closed," he said, shaking out the cape and folding it neatly. "I close up early on most nights. Tonight was a favor for a special client."

He winked at his client and ushered him toward the exit, accepting payment en route.

When he returned, Angus stepped closer, his eyes fixed on the barber.

"We've received information that suggests illegal poker games are being run from the back of your shop. One of these games supposedly took place the night of the attack. What do you know about that?"

The barber's eyes widened in surprise, and he shook his head.

"That's ridiculous! I don't know anything about that, Sheriff. I run a clean business here."

Angus studied the man's eyes, failing to see any glimmer of deceit in them.

"Does anyone else work here besides you?"

The barber paused briefly before he answered.

"Fifteen years I've had this shop, Sheriff, and I've never needed anyone else's help. I've worked here every single day since the day I opened those doors. On my own, just me. And I've never had anyone complain or cause trouble. Like I said, I run a clean business."

"I'm not here to insult you, sir. Just trying to do my job. What about your keys? Is it possible someone has access to your keys and let himself in?"

Again, the shop owner paused, his eyes revealing that his mind was churning.

"My nephew sometimes helps with cleaning up after I close but there's no way he would be involved in anything illegal. No way."

"Do you know if he was here the night the attack happened in the alley behind your shop?"

Once again, the barber paused, the look in his eyes telling Angus that he was facing a moral dilemma.

"Yes, he was here the night of the assault, but he's an honest boy, Sheriff. He's in for an hour every week to clean then locks up and leaves. That's it. When you meet him, you'll see for yourself. He's a bright young man helping out his uncle. In fact, you can ask him yourself. He should be arriving any minute now."

Angus nodded, sensing the barber's sincerity.

"I'll wait for him if you don't mind."

The barber nodded and gestured for Angus to sit in one of his chairs before he busied himself with sweeping the floor, the concern on his face evident.

# CHAPTER THIRTEEN

Angus took a seat in the waiting area, his gaze drifting to the framed photographs and certificates on the walls. He heard the door chime and turned to see a young boy, no older than fifteen, stepping inside. The boy's eyes widened when he saw Angus, and he froze for a moment before turning to bolt back out the door.

"Hey! Stop!" Angus shouted, jumping to his feet.

Miguel, who had been watching from outside, sprang into action. He grabbed the boy by the arm just as he tried to dart past, holding him firmly.

"Let me go!" the boy yelled, struggling against Miguel's grip.

"It's okay, kid. We just want to talk," Miguel said calmly, leading him back inside.

The barber's face had gone pale, and he quickly closed the door behind them.

The boy's eyes were wide with fear, and he looked from his uncle to Angus, clearly terrified.

"I didn't do anything wrong!" he blurted.

"Relax, son. We just need some answers," Angus said, trying to reassure him. "What's your name?"

"Ali," the boy replied, his voice shaking.

"All right, Ali," Angus continued. "We know you were here the night of the attack in the alley behind the shop. I don't think I need to tell you how important it is that you tell me if you heard or saw anything, right?"

Ali hesitated, his eyes darting to his uncle, who gave him an encouraging nod.

"I was just cleaning up like always. One night a few months ago, these men showed up. They told me to let them use the back room for a poker game. Said they would pay me a lot of money to stay quiet and leave them alone. So, I did. I figured it wasn't hurting anyone. It was just a game of poker, and the money is really good. Since they put my father on those kidney machines, he's not able to do any work so I only did it to help my parents."

The boy wiped a stray tear from his cheek.

"I'm sorry, Uncle. I didn't mean to get you into any trouble. I was only trying to help *baba* with the bills."

Angus exchanged a glance with Miguel.

"What did these men look like? Did you recognize any of them? Names?"

Ali shook his head.

"They don't come here for their hair or anything, so I

didn't recognize them, and they've never told me their names either. But one of them had a fancy black car. He's the one who's in charge, the one who tells them to pay me."

"Did you see the attack or hear anything else that night?" Miguel asked, his tone gentle.

Ali nodded slowly.

"I heard a commotion outside, like someone was fighting. I heard a woman scream, but I was too scared to look. I didn't want any trouble, so I just stayed inside until they left."

Angus sighed, feeling the weight of the boy's fear and the gravity of the situation.

"Thank you, Ali. You've been very helpful so far. Now, do you remember anything else about the car or the men?"

Ali thought for a moment, then shook his head again.

"No, just that the car was really nice. And the man who's in charge always dresses really well."

"How do you mean?" Angus probed.

"He wears really expensive clothes. All the top brands like Armani, Gucci, Boss, you know. Like the movie stars."

"That's very helpful, Ali, thank you. One more thing - how do they make contact with you to arrange these poker games?"

The boy shrugged his shoulders.

"They don't. It's never on the same night. I just have to

make sure I'm here at nine every night. If they're not here, then I can leave."

Angus nodded, then turned to the barber.

"Thank you for your cooperation. We're going to need to keep an eye on things here. If anything else comes up, please let us know immediately. And I'd take away the boy's key if I were you, sir. Keep him out of sight and away from the shop until we have this all straightened out. I'll have a patrol car keep an eye out for the men tonight."

The barber nodded, his face still pale.

"Of course, Sheriff. Anything to help, and I give you my word that my nephew won't be doing anything like this again. I'll be locking up the shop myself every night. Like I said, I run a clean business and I intend to keep it that way."

As they left the barbershop, Miguel whispered to Angus. "You're just going to let this kid go, Sheriff?"

Angus turned to face him.

"He's a kid who made a bad decision to help his family out. A poor judgment call, that's it. I'll call on him if we need more evidence to prove Jack Travis was here that night. But for now, our priority is to keep him out of harm's way and find Hannah before it's too late."

Angus turned and walked back toward his vehicle with Miguel falling in step beside him.

"You think it was Travis who paid the kid off?" Miguel asked.

"I do, yes, which is why we need to tread carefully."

"So, why aren't we bringing Travis in for questioning? I mean, we think he was the one who attacked Hannah in the alley the other night. We have the kid who can testify that he was here. He's our most likely suspect right now, isn't he? Even that Vincent guy said Travis had found out that Hannah was a reporter. That gives him motive and opportunity." Miguel's voice was urgent.

"It's all circumstantial, Miguel. Hearsay. We need proof that he attacked Hannah. Then, once we find her, we need more evidence to prove that he kidnapped her with the intention to finish what he started. A guy like Jack Travis will lawyer up before we even get as far as sitting him down in the interrogation room. We need to do this right. We'll have one chance at bringing him down, so we cannot slip up. Travis cannot know we're onto him."

"But what if he has Hannah locked up somewhere right now and is about to kill her? We can stop him."

"We keep praying that he doesn't, Miguel. We don't even know for certain if she is really missing or that Travis took her. She could be sitting feet-up at her father's house right now for all we know. As much as I want to go charging after Travis, we need to explore that possibility first."

But as Angus slipped behind the wheel of his truck, momentarily appeasing Miguel, he couldn't shake the feeling that they were about to dive into something much deeper and more dangerous than they had anticipated. Yet he knew one thing for certain: they were on the right track, and they wouldn't stop until they found Hannah and uncovered the truth behind what was really going on behind the walls of The Grande.

Ali's information about the fancy black car and the mysterious man was a valuable lead. They had to keep pushing forward, no matter what danger lay ahead.

He switched his vehicle into reverse and pointed the truck's nose toward Hannah's father's house, silently praying that they would find her there.

# CHAPTER FOURTEEN

The drive was tense, and the quiet streets of Weyport felt ominous with the weight of their investigation. Angus's mind raced as he thought about their next steps if Hannah wasn't there. Every second they wasted was a second she remained missing.

And the stakes couldn't be higher.

As they pulled up to a modest house in the center of town, Angus turned to Miguel.

"Let's make this quick. We only need to know if Hannah's here or if her father has heard from her or seen anything unusual. Let's not give him any unnecessary cause for concern until we know more. Unless the situation warrants it."

"Copy that, Sheriff," Miguel replied.

They walked up the weed-edged path to the front door and Angus knocked firmly. After a few moments, the door creaked open, revealing a weary-looking man wearing stained gray tracksuit pants and a white tank top. He was loosely holding a beer in one hand, his unshaven face and disheveled appearance suggesting he hadn't bathed in a while.

"Mr. Jackson?" Angus asked.

"Yes, that's me," he replied, concern and annoyance in his voice. "Is this about Hannah? What's she done now again? She's always poking her nose where it doesn't belong."

"Sheriff Reid, and this is Deputy Garcia," Angus introduced himself before he continued.

"That's why we're here, yes," Angus said gently. "We're trying to find Hannah and thought she might be here."

"I would be so lucky," her father replied sarcastically.

"Have you heard from her recently?" Angus asked.

Mr. Jackson shook his head, taking a swig from his beer.

"Why would I?"

"She's your daughter, is she not?" Angus verified.

"Since when does that mean anything? She doesn't tell me her ins and outs, Sheriff. She's too busy trying to get as far away from me and this town as possible. But for what it's worth, no, I haven't. Last I saw her, was when I bumped into her at the gas station. Didn't even remember it was my birthday. Said she was working on some big story and that she was in a hurry. She had that excited twinkle in her eyes, but wouldn't tell me anything. Said it was too dangerous. Imagine!" He scoffed and rolled his eyes.

Angus exchanged a glance with Miguel.

"When was this, Mr. Jackson?" Angus asked.

"About two weeks ago. She's always making up some story to impress me. Likes to embellish things, if you know what I mean?"

"Two weeks ago. You haven't spoken to her since?" Miguel queried.

Mr. Jackson looked directly at them.

"It's not that strange, you know. If it weren't for our monthly dinners, I'd never see her. She tries to get out of them all the time, says she's too busy with work, but it never flies with me. So, she comes just to shut me up. I keep telling her, a woman's place is at home, not chasing after stories nobody cares about anyway. She should be at home, raising kids, and taking care of a husband. Not running after big city lights and fancy offices like her mother did when she decided to up and leave me with a bratty tween. But Hannah's never been one to take instructions from me. Always thinks she's destined for more. She's just like her mother."

He turned and walked into a messy living room and plopped down in a dirty La-Z-Boy, kicking it back to recline as he took another large sip of his beer. Angus noticed the bitterness in his voice.

"So, you haven't heard from her since, Mr. Jackson? Any calls, messages, anything?" Angus pushed.

Mr. Jackson sighed and put down his beer.

"She left a cryptic voice message on my phone the other night. Made it sound all important like she was some secret spy or something. She said if she didn't make it to dinner next week, the story probably got the better of her. No way I'm falling for it," his chuckle almost immediately turned into a phlegmy cough. He washed it down with another few sips of beer.

"Did she mention anyone she was meeting? Any names, places?"

"She's always very secretive about her work," he grumbled, "so imagine my surprise when she mentioned she was meeting some guy in a warehouse and that she'd finally be able to make me proud." He looked down, his eyes softening momentarily before hardening again.

"Can we hear that message?" Angus asked.

Mr. Jackson nodded, retrieving his phone from a cluttered side table. He played the message, and Angus and Miguel listened intently.

*"HEY DAD, it's Hannah. I know we don't talk much, but I just wanted you to know I'm onto something big. I think it's finally going to make you proud of me. Anyway, if I don't make it to our next dinner, it means the story got the better of me. I'm meeting a guy at a warehouse tonight. I can't tell you more right now, but you'll understand soon. Take care."*

. . .

THE MESSAGE ENDED, leaving a heavy silence in its wake. Angus's mind raced with the implications.

"Do you have any idea which warehouse she was talking about?" Miguel asked.

Mr. Jackson shook his head.

"No idea. You heard it yourselves. She obviously didn't say. Like I said, she was just trying to impress me by making it sound all secretive. Always making up elaborate stories to get out of our dinners."

Angus nodded.

"Mr. Jackson, there's no easy way to say this, but your daughter was attacked a few nights ago and has since been reported missing."

The room fell silent as Angus watched her father's face turn to worry.

"Missing? Attacked? I had no idea. She's okay though, isn't she?"

"Although she survived the attack, she is still missing. We're doing everything we can to find her, Mr. Jackson, but if you hear from Hannah, by any means, please contact me right away."

Hannah's father nodded as Angus handed him a business card before adding, "Thank you for your time, Mr. Jackson. We'll see ourselves out."

As they headed back to the truck, Miguel spoke up.

"That was so sad to witness."

"Which part?"

"All of it! Hannah's dad thinks so little of her. His

disdain for her and his slovenly behavior toward her career. It's no wonder she tries to get out of their dinners. But it always takes two to tango, doesn't it? I mean, she forgot her own father's birthday. I've always known Hannah to be a pushy, hardworking reporter and all, but putting ambition ahead of family to the point where you forget your father's birthday. That's not something you see where I come from."

"I guess people get their wires crossed when it comes to chasing after success. Pride comes before the fall, right?"

Miguel agreed with a saintly "Amen" before he jumped back into discussing the case.

"The warehouse district near the docks seems like a good place to start. It's known for being a hotspot for shady deals. If Travis took her, it would be a great place to keep her locked up since most of the warehouses are vacant this time of year."

"Agreed," Angus replied, determination etched on his face. "That's precisely where we're heading next."

The drive was filled with tense silence. Angus's thoughts kept drifting back to Hannah's message. The urgency in her voice suggested she had been close to something significant. But that also suggested that she was in grave danger.

# CHAPTER FIFTEEN

I t was already late when they arrived at the old warehouse district near the docks, a maze of abandoned buildings and rusting shipping containers. The area was eerily quiet, the air thick with the briny scent of saltwater mixed with the lingering, pungent odor of decaying marine life. Angus and Miguel parked the truck and began to explore the network of narrow streets and alleys.

"This is going to be like finding a needle in a haystack, Miguel. Keep your eyes peeled for anything unusual," Angus instructed.

They moved cautiously, their flashlights cutting through the darkness. The sound of their footsteps echoed off the walls, adding to the sense of foreboding. After a few hours, they came across a warehouse with its door slightly ajar. Angus motioned for Miguel to follow as he pushed the door open and stepped inside.

The interior was dimly lit, the only light coming from a few flickering bulbs strung haphazardly across the ceiling. The space was cluttered with old machinery and stacks of wooden crates. The beam from Angus's flashlight swept across the room, revealing signs of recent activity—a half-empty coffee cup, cigarette butts, and a discarded jacket.

"Someone's been here recently," Miguel observed, carefully lifting the jacket with the back of his flashlight.

"Stay alert," Angus whispered. "We don't know who or what we're dealing with."

Hands on their holstered guns, they moved deeper into the warehouse, their senses heightened. The flickering light cast eerie shadows on the walls, and every gritty crunch of loose dirt under their shoes made them more tense. At the far end of the room, Angus noticed a door that was slightly ajar.

"Over here," he said quietly, motioning for Miguel to follow.

Angus's heart pounded in his chest as he pushed the door open slowly, revealing a small office space. A laptop sat open but dormant atop an otherwise empty desk. The screen had been smashed.

A sudden noise from the adjacent room made them both jump. Angus signaled for Miguel to stay back as he cautiously moved toward the source of the sound. He pushed open yet another door, and his flashlight illuminated a grim scene.

On the floor lay the lifeless body of a man. A dark stain spread across his chest where he had been shot. The sight sent a chill down Angus's spine.

As he shone his flashlight into the dark space in search of danger, Miguel stepped into the room behind him and knelt beside the body.

"He's dead."

Angus swallowed hard, his mind racing.

"Think it's the guy Hannah was meeting?" Miguel whispered.

"I think that's highly probable. The better questions are, was he dead before she arrived, or was he killed while she was meeting with him?"

The air in the room felt, charged with the remnants of violence.

"Keep looking, Miguel. She might be in hiding."

He intentionally forced his mind not to think of the alternative.

Miguel stood, his expression stony.

"What if Travis and his men come back? They could be watching us right now."

Angus nodded, the gravity of their situation pressing down on him.

"If this was his doing and he took Hannah, he already has what he came for."

Moving slowly and quietly through the rest of the space, there was no evidence of Hannah having been there.

"She's not here," Miguel stated the obvious.

"Agreed. Probably gulls that made the noise. Call it in, Miguel," Angus instructed.

But as they turned to go back toward the dead body, the faint sound of footsteps echoed from the far end of the warehouse. Angus and Miguel exchanged a tense glance, their hands instinctively moving back to their weapons.

"Stay close and stay quiet," Angus whispered, leading the way back through the maze of machinery and crates.

The footsteps grew louder, and Angus's heart raced.

He peeked around a corner, spotting the silhouette of a man moving cautiously through the shadows. He motioned for Miguel to stay back and slowly drew his gun.

"Who's there?" Angus called out, his voice steady despite the tension.

The figure froze, and for a moment, the warehouse fell silent. Then, in a blur of motion, the man bolted towards the exit.

"Stop!" Miguel shouted, giving chase.

Angus followed close behind, their footsteps echoing off the walls as they pursued the man through the labyrinthine corridors of the warehouse district. The suspect darted around corners, trying to lose them, but Angus and Miguel were relentless.

Finally, they cornered him in a dead-end alley. The man turned, his eyes wide with fear.

"Don't shoot!" he pleaded, raising his hands.

Angus approached cautiously, keeping his gun trained on the man.

"Who are you? What are you doing here?"

The man swallowed hard, his eyes darting nervously between Angus and Miguel.

"I'm just a lookout. I swear, I didn't hurt anyone."

Miguel stepped forward, his expression fierce.

"Who are you working for? Is it Jack Travis?"

The man hesitated, then slowly shook his head.

"I don't know who that is. I just watch the place, that's all."

"Who pays you to watch the place?" Angus tried to control the urgency in his voice but needed answers, and fast.

"The dead guy."

Angus felt a surge of frustration.

"What about the girl? The reporter. Did you see her? Where is she?"

"I don't know, man. I swear!" the lookout insisted.

"I came to collect my money and found him dead on the floor. That's all I know! He was alive when I left yesterday. I swear, man. I didn't kill him. I wouldn't. I've been his lookout for a year and he's paid me good money. Why would I kill him?"

"Who was he? What's his name?" Angus pressed.

The scrawny lookout's body was visibly shaking now.

"Shadow, his name is Shadow. I don't know his real name."

Angus exchanged a glance with Miguel.

"We need to verify this. If he's telling the truth, Hannah could still be alive."

Miguel nodded.

"I'll call for backup and get him back to the station for questioning. Maybe he knows more than he's letting on."

The lookout whined proclaiming his innocence as Miguel cuffed him. After Miguel secured him to a nearby post, he hurried back to where Angus stood over the murdered man, the tension thick in the air. Angus felt a mixture of hope and dread. Though they were closer to finding Hannah, the danger was escalating with every step they took.

While Miguel called the station, Angus dialed Dr. Murphy Delaney's number, hoping that her initial findings might point them in the right direction.

# CHAPTER SIXTEEN

W ithin half an hour, Murphy arrived at the scene, her demeanor professional but her eyes showing the warmth of her friendship with Angus.

"Why is it that your bodies mostly show up in the middle of the night or at the crack of dawn, Reid? A girl needs her beauty sleep, you know?" she said as a greeting, giving him a brief smile.

"Probably because everyone knows your beauty is already off the charts, Murph," Angus said, returning her smile.

"Careful, flattery will get you everywhere right now," she quipped before turning her attention back to the body at their feet. "So, out with it. What do you have for me tonight?"

"A dead man named Shadow, apparently. He was

somehow tied up in Hannah's investigation," Angus replied.

"Hannah Jackson? From the *Herald*?"

"Sadly, yes."

"I see." Murphy looked around. "Is she okay?"

"We're certainly praying that she is. She's been reported missing and the trail of breadcrumbs has led me to this guy. I'm hoping you can give me something that might help us find her, Murph. Time is of the essence."

Murphy nodded, her eyes scanning the scene.

"I will certainly try my best. I like Hannah. She's tenacious. Reminds me of myself when I thought the world revolved around my career."

She crouched beside the body, her gloved hands gently examining the wound.

"Single gunshot wound to the chest. Close range, judging by the burn marks around the entry wound."

"Any idea on the time of death?" Angus asked, his voice steady but filled with anticipation.

Murphy took the body's liver temperature, glanced at her watch as she did her calculations, and reported back.

"Based on the lividity and body temperature, I'd estimate he's been dead at least twenty-four hours. I'll know for sure once I get him back to the lab."

As she worked, Murphy's eyes were sharp and focused.

"He took a beating to the face, and there's some

bruising on his knuckles, defensive wounds most likely. He fought back."

She carefully pulled away the sleeves of Shadow's t-shirt.

"He was held by force. See here?" She pointed to the bruises around his biceps. "I'll have to take a closer look under the lights, but my initial thoughts are that there were two people holding him. The one who gripped his right arm had much bigger hands."

"How big?" Miguel asked from where he was quietly observing the scene.

"Bigger than your average man."

"Anything else?" Angus asked, stepping closer.

Murphy looked thoughtful.

"There's something under his fingernails. Could be skin, maybe hair. I'll have to analyze it in the lab, but it might give us more clues about his attacker. I'll put it under the microscope the second we get the body on my table."

Angus watched her work, admiration in his eyes. Despite the severity of the situation, he couldn't help but feel a fondness toward her. They had always had a connection, a mutual respect and endearment that went beyond professional boundaries.

"I'll try not to wake you with the next murder, Murphy," Angus teased, trying to lighten the mood.

She smirked, glancing up at him.

"Sleep is overrated. Besides, who else is going to solve your cases?"

He chuckled.

"Touché. Thanks for coming out here so quickly."

"Anything for you, Angus," she replied, her tone sincere.

As she finished her initial examination, she stood up, removing her gloves. "I'll get the body back to the lab and run a full analysis. I'll let you know as soon as I have more information."

"Thanks, Murphy. We appreciate it," Angus said.

She gave him a reassuring smile before turning to her team, who had just arrived to transport the body.

Miguel watched her leave, then turned to Angus.

"She's good at what she does."

"The best," Angus agreed. "And a good friend."

"Seems like more than just a friend," Miguel said with a knowing look.

Angus shook his head, a small smile playing on his lips. "Let's focus on finding Hannah, shall we?"


WITH MURPHY'S team handling the body, Angus and Miguel turned their attention back to the warehouse. Finding any clues that might lead them to Hannah was of vital importance.

As they searched the room, Miguel spotted something

on the floor near a stack of crates. He bent down and picked up a small piece of torn fabric.

"Looks like it could be from a jacket," he said, handing it to Angus.

Angus examined the fabric closely then dropped it in an evidence bag. "Let's show it to Clara Matthews first thing in the morning. Perhaps she can confirm if it's from one of Hannah's jackets before we send it off for DNA testing. It'll save us some much needed time. If it matches any of her clothing, it confirms that she was here meeting this Shadow guy."

Miguel nodded, soberly.

"Which means Travis was likely here too."

Angus felt a surge of determination as they continued their search, finding more signs of a struggle. Remnants from broken wooden crates were scattered across the floor, and a chair was overturned. He mentally pieced together what had happened.

Miguel's voice broke through his thoughts.

"Sheriff, over here."

Angus turned to see Miguel standing near a set of tire tracks leading out of the back of the warehouse.

"These could be from the car that took Hannah," Miguel suggested.

Angus nodded, following the tracks with his flashlight.

"Let's see where they lead."

They traced the tracks through the narrow dirt alleyways of the warehouse district, their footsteps muffled in the silence. The tracks eventually led them to a secluded area behind another warehouse, where they abruptly stopped.

Angus shone his flashlight over the ground, turning around in search of the original tracks. But the tire tracks were messy, indicating that there was more than one vehicle that went through the area.

"This is where they must have switched vehicles," Angus said, frustration evident in his voice.

Miguel sighed.

"They're covering their tracks well. Pardon the pun."

"These guys are smart, Miguel. This wasn't their first rodeo."

Angus's phone buzzed, breaking the silence. He answered quickly and heard Murphy's voice on the other end.

"Angus, I've got preliminary results," she announced.

"That was quick," Angus replied pressing the phone closer to his ear.

"I got on it the moment we got here. The substance under Shadow's fingernails is definitely skin. I'm running it through a DNA sequencer now. If we're lucky, we'll have enough to feed into CODIS to see if we get a match, but that will take time. I've also taken the victim's prints to establish his identity."

"Thanks, Murph, that's a great find. Keep us posted," Angus replied, feeling a glimmer of hope.

He hung up and turned to Miguel.

"Murphy's running tests on the skin she found under Shadow's nails. She's also running his prints. Hopefully we not only find out his true identity, we also get a lead on who attacked him."

Miguel nodded. "Let's hope it's sooner rather than later."

BACK AT THE CRIME SCENE, Angus checked in with the forensics team, who hadn't found any more leads, except the broken laptop.

"Any way to get this thing working again?" he asked one of the men.

"It's not just the screen that was damaged, Sheriff. The hard drive is fried. Looks like they poured vinegar on it. Whoever it was knew what they were doing. They went all out to make sure nothing could be retrieved. It's a long shot, a very long shot, but I'll do my best to resuscitate it."

AS ANGUS and Miguel made their way back to the truck, the findings swirled in Angus's head. The longer he sat with the facts of the case, the more confusing they became. Who was the murder victim and why was Hannah meeting with him? Did he protect Hannah only to get killed for his heroism? Or was Hannah dealt the same fate and her body would be the next one discovered?

# CHAPTER SEVENTEEN

The morning sun filtered through the blinds of Angus's office, casting long shadows across the room. Clara Matthews sat opposite him, her face pale and drawn with worry. On the desk between them lay an evidence bag containing the small piece of torn fabric that had been found in the warehouse. Next to it, the diamond found in the alley.

"What's in the evidence bags?" Clara asked, her eyes pinned to the labeled plastic bags across from her.

"That's why I called you here. We need your help identifying these," Angus began, his voice gentle but insistent. He placed them side by side in front of her. "We believe this to be a piece of fabric and this one, possibly a diamond earring. Do you recognize either?"

Clara picked up each evidence bag, her hands trembling slightly as she examined the items. Moments later, she tossed the bag with the diamond aside, her eyes fixed on the piece of khaki fabric. Tears welled up in her eyes as she nodded slowly.

"Yes, this is from Hannah's jacket. One of those safari jackets. I gave it to her last Christmas. She said she looked like Hercule Poirot. You know, the character from the Agatha Christie novels. She wore it all the time," Clara whispered, her voice breaking as she pushed the evidence bag across the desk.

Angus and Miguel exchanged a look, the confirmation hitting them hard.

"And the diamond?" Angus asked.

She shook her head, fighting hard to contain her tears.

"Clara, we need to fill you in on everything we've found so far," Angus said carefully. "We've been to her father's house. He hadn't seen Hannah and didn't know where she was. He did have a voice message from her, though. She sounded worried, like she was in over her head. She mentioned meeting someone in a warehouse and that she'd finally be able to make her father proud."

Clara's eyes widened in shock.

"That man! He has always denigrated her. It's no wonder she wants to get out of here. Did she really sound like she was in over her head? I didn't know things had gotten that serious. I mean, yes, there was the attack in the alley, but she'd made it sound like it was nothing to worry about. She must have been really scared to leave a message like that on her father's phone. She would never give him the satisfaction of thinking he was right about her. She'd rather die than..."

She stopped from finishing her sentence, instantly realizing the reality of her words.

Angus nodded, his expression grave.

"We followed that lead to the warehouse district. When we got there, we found signs of a struggle and a man named Shadow. He was dead, shot in the chest. We think he was the one Hannah was meeting."

Clara gasped, her hand flying to her mouth.

"She's not—"

"We only found Shadow," Angus said.

"Poor Hannah. Do you think she saw the murder?" Clara continued.

"It's possible," Miguel interjected. "We think she might have been taken by the same people who killed Shadow. We're trying to piece together what happened."

"And if this piece of fabric is in fact from Hannah's jacket, she put up a fight," Angus continued. "Take another look, Clara. We need you to be sure before we send it off for DNA testing. Timing is everything right now, and if we can get a head start, it would help save time. If it matches, it means Hannah was definitely at the warehouse."

Clara took another look at the fabric sample then nodded.

"It's definitely from her jacket. Look." She pulled out

her phone and tapped the screen a few times before holding up a photo of the two of them together.

Clara's eyes filled with tears again.

"She loves that jacket. Please, you have to find her. I'll do whatever I can to help. I just can't believe this is happening. Hannah was always so careful."

Angus nodded, forcing his emotions aside so as to not get the better of him.

"Do you know why she would meet someone like Shadow?" Angus asked gently. "Did she mention anything about her investigation that might explain it?"

Clara shook her head, wiping her eyes. "She never mentioned him to me. She was very secretive about her sources, always wanting to protect them. She just said she was really close to finding what we needed to expose Duncan Steele. I should have pulled her off the story, but she insisted. If I had, then Hannah would still be here."

"You're not to blame, Clara. Let's focus on bringing her home rather than on what ifs," Angus said, silently praying that he wasn't getting her hopes up for nothing.

Miguel leaned forward, his expression intense.

"What about a man named Lucas? Did she ever mention him?"

Clara frowned, shaking her head again.

"No, I don't know any Lucas. Hannah keeps a lot to herself, especially when she thinks an investigation could jeopardize the paper or the story. She holds her cards close to her chest until she has enough facts to support her articles."

Angus reached across the desk, placing a comforting hand on Clara's. "We're doing everything we can to find her. We won't stop until we do."

Clara nodded as fresh tears filled her eyes.

"Please, Angus, find her. She's like a daughter to me. I can't bear the thought of losing her."

"We will, Clara," Angus promised. "We're following every lead, and we'll find her, Clara," Angus promised.

Clara took a deep breath, trying to steady herself.

"Thank you. I trust you, Angus. Just please, find her."

"We will," Miguel echoed. "You have our word."

WITH CLARA'S confirmation on record that Hannah was present at the warehouse, Miguel walked her outside.

Angus studied the information in the case file on his desk, feeling a renewed sense of resolve. They had to keep pushing forward, one piece of evidence at a time, no matter what danger lay ahead.

His thoughts were interrupted a few minutes later when Murphy confidently strode into the room, holding a folder filled with her findings.

"I've got some good news," she said, handing the folder to Angus. "We got a match on the skin sample. It belongs to a known associate of Jack Travis—a man named Derek Holt."

Angus's eyes widened.

"Holt? He's one of Travis's top enforcers."

Murphy nodded as Angus's fingers worked his computer's keyboard to bring up Holt's file.

"Assault and battery, burglary, auto theft—he's got a serious RAP sheet. And wouldn't you know it? The guy's six foot four. I bet he has a pair of hands to match his height."

"I would agree. I'll even go as far as saying I'd probably be able to match his handprint to the bruises on Shadow's arm."

"If Holt was the one who killed Shadow, then Travis is definitely behind this."

"Are you going to arrest him?" Murphy asked. "The epithelial sample is evidence enough, isn't it?"

"It certainly proves that Holt came in contact with Shadow. Is it enough to prove that he pulled the trigger? Probably not, but I'm definitely going to bring him in for questioning. With some divine intervention he might turn on his employer and tell us where Hannah is."

Angus felt a surge of energy.

"What did I miss?" Miguel asked as he walked back into the office, immediately picking up on the elevated mood. He looked at Murphy then Angus.

"The skin under Shadow's nails belongs to Derek Holt."

"So, Jack Travis is behind this," Miguel said darkly,

immediately recognizing the name. "We have enough to bring him in."

Angus nodded before he turned to Murphy.

"Anything on who this Shadow guy was?"

Murphy shook her head.

"Nothing. CODIS came up empty on his fingerprints, which is rather strange. I'm running his DNA now."

"Thanks, Murphy," Angus said, giving her a grateful smile. "I'd be nowhere without your help."

"Just doing my job," she replied, returning his smile. "Be careful out there, Angus. You too, Miguel."

"We will," Angus said, watching as she walked away.

Turning back to Miguel, Angus felt a renewed sense of direction with the case.

"Let's track down Derek Holt first. There's still no evidence to prove that Travis was there."

Angus turned back and grabbed his jacket from the back of his chair before snatching his truck keys from his desk drawer.

"Any luck on Ross Mead, the guy from The Black Cat?"

"As a matter of fact, yes. He's dead. Has been for nearly fifteen years." Miguel paused briefly before continuing. "And before you ask me if I'm sure the answer is yes, I ran my checks twice. Got a death certificate and everything. My guess is our mystery man helped himself to the real Ross Mead's identity."

"Which tells me that he has something to hide," Angus

said. "Let's get Holt then see if we can find out more about who this Lucas guy is. I have a hunch he and Mead are one and the same."

With fortitude etched on their faces, Angus and Miguel set out to find Derek Holt, knowing that every second counted in their race to find Hannah and bring the culprits to justice.

# CHAPTER EIGHTEEN

As Angus and Miguel drove through the narrow streets of Weyport, uneasiness flitted between them. The sun had fully risen and was casting sharp shadows across the town. The address they had for Derek Holt was one town over, a rundown bungalow in a quiet part of town. Angus's thoughts were a whirlwind, each one laced with the urgent need to find Hannah before it was too late. His gut told him they were getting closer, but that also meant the danger was escalating.

"Keep your eyes open," Angus instructed Miguel, his voice steady but filled with an undercurrent of tension. "Holt's not going to come quietly. He'll run the second he knows we're closing in."

The truck came to a slow stop in front of the dilapidated building, paint peeling from its walls and windows covered with blankets. The neighborhood was eerily quiet, save for the distant hum of traffic and the occasional bark of a dog.

As they exited the vehicle, Angus scanned the surroundings, noting the narrow alleyways and rusted fences that created a winding network between the dilapidated properties. It was the perfect place for someone like Holt to hide. An even better place to keep Hannah locked up. But it also offered numerous escape routes.

"Be alert," Angus said, leading the way up the creaky wooden porch steps. The porch was worn, the smell of mildew and old garbage hanging in the air. Each step they took echoed into the silence, a stark reminder of how exposed they were.

They reached Holt's door, and Angus motioned for Miguel to take the other side. He knocked firmly, the sound muffled by the old wood. There was no answer. He knocked again, harder this time.

"Derek Holt! This is Sheriff Reid! Open up!"

Silence.

Angus exchanged a look with Miguel before drawing his gun. He nodded, and Miguel kicked the door in. The door swung open with a crash, revealing a sparsely furnished room. The air was stale, and it was clear it had not been cleaned recently.

"Clear," Miguel called from the kitchen area.

Angus moved into the living room, his eyes scanning for any signs of recent activity. Newspapers were scattered across the coffee table, and a half-eaten sandwich covered in mold sat on the counter. But it was the open window at the back of the small house that caught his attention.

"He's on the run," Angus muttered, frustration gnawing at him. "He must have seen us coming."

"Sheriff! Over here!" Miguel's voice rang out from the bedroom.

Angus hurried over, finding Miguel holding a cell phone he had retrieved from under the bed.

"It's still on," Miguel said, handing it to Angus.

Angus took the phone, scrolling through the recent messages. One caught his eye—a message from an unknown number, received just half an hour ago:

*"You're compromised. Get out now."*

"SOMEONE TIPPED HIM OFF. We need to move fast. He can't have gone far."

They sprinted back to the car, the pressure of the situation spurring them on. As they peeled out of the parking lot, Angus dialed the station, instructing them to put an APB on Holt. His mind was a blur of possibilities, each one more dire than the last.

"Where do you think he's headed?" Miguel asked, his

eyes scanning the streets as they sped through the town.

"His file mentioned he owned a small fishing boat. If I were Holt, I'd be looking for a quick escape route—someplace I could lay low until things cooled down," Angus replied. "Let's head back toward the docks. There are plenty of places to hide there, and he might try to get on his boat out of there."

The drive to the docks was tense, every minute feeling like an eternity. Angus's thoughts drifted back to Hannah, her voice on the phone message filled with a mix of determination and fear. They had to find her. Failure was not an option.

As they approached the small harbor, the maritime landscape came into view—cranes towered over fishing trawlers lining the waterfront, fishing baskets swayed with the afternoon catch and the smell of fish was heavy in the air. It was a place filled with shadows and hiding spots, perfect for someone like Holt.

"Over there," Miguel pointed, spotting a tall figure darting along the harbor wall.

Angus hit the gas, the truck lurching forward as they closed the distance. Holt glanced over his shoulder, his eyes widening in panic before he took off at a sprint.

"Go around the other side! Cut him off!" Angus shouted, veering the truck toward one side of the marina while Miguel jumped out and ran toward the other.

Adrenaline flowed through Angus as he navigated the narrow alleyways, the truck's tires screeching on the asphalt. He could see Holt ahead, weaving through the maze of fishmongers offloading their catch. Angus skidded to a stop, jumping out of the car and giving chase on foot.

The sound of heavy breathing and pounding footsteps filled the air. Angus's mind was laser-focused, every sense heightened as he closed in on Holt. They rounded a corner, and Angus could see Miguel coming from the opposite direction, effectively trapping Holt between them.

"Derek Holt! Stop!" Angus yelled, his voice echoing in the salty air.

Holt glanced around desperately, realizing he was cornered. In a last-ditch effort, he scrambled up a stack of abandoned lobster cages, his hands and feet finding purchase on the rusted metal.

Angus huffed a breath in annoyance and followed him. The climb was precarious, the metal slick with moisture from the nearby sea. But Angus's determination pushed him forward, each movement deliberate and focused.

Miguel followed suit, the two of them scaling the pile of wired metal and mangled fishing nets with practiced ease. Holt reached the top, panting heavily, and looked around for an escape route. There was none. He turned to face them, his eyes wild with fear and defiance.

"It's over, Holt!" Angus shouted, his gun trained on the man. "There's nowhere to go. Come down, and we'll talk."

Holt's eyes darted around, the panic evident. He took a step back, and his foot slipped slightly on the edge of one of the cages.

"You don't understand! They'll kill me if I go with you!"

"Who? Travis?" Miguel asked, his gun also trained on Holt. "We can protect you, but you need to come with us now!"

Holt hesitated, the fear in his eyes warring with the instinct to survive. "You can't protect me from him. No one can."

Angus took a cautious step forward, his voice steady.

"We can try, Derek. But you need to give us something. Where is Hannah?"

Holt's eyes flickered with something that looked like regret.

"I don't know. I swear, I don't know. I was just following orders."

"Whose orders?" Angus pressed, desperate for more information. "Where did you take her?"

Before Holt could answer, a gunshot rang out, the sound deafening in the narrow space. Holt's eyes widened in shock as a crimson stain spread across his chest. He stumbled, his body teetering on the edge before he fell, hitting the ground below with a sickening thud.

"Gunman! Get down!" Miguel shouted and pulled Angus down behind the cages.

# CHAPTER NINETEEN

The sound of their ragged breathing filled the silence. Angus realized with dismay that someone didn't want Holt to talk, and he was willing to kill to ensure his silence.

"We need to move," Miguel ordered. "They'll be coming for us next."

Angus nodded, his mind already calculating their next move.

"We need to find that sniper. He's our next lead."

They moved cautiously, using the pile of lobster cages and nets for cover as they made their way around. The sense of danger was palpable, every shadow a potential threat. Angus's thoughts were a whirlwind of anger, fear, and resolve. They were so close, yet it felt like the goalpost kept moving.

As they rounded a pile of crates, Angus spotted a flash

of movement in the distance—a figure darting between the boat houses.

"There! That's our shooter!"

They gave chase, the scene unfolding like a high-stakes action movie. The person was fast, weaving through the maze of fishmonger sheds with practiced agility. The chase led them through narrow alleyways, across rickety docks, and over piles of abandoned equipment. The maritime setting was a labyrinth of metal and shadows, each twist and turn adding to the intensity of the pursuit.

Angus and Miguel pushed themselves to the limit, their breaths coming in heavy gasps as they closed the distance.

They rounded a corner, and the figure was within reach. Angus lunged, tackling the person to the ground. The impact was hard, the sound of their bodies hitting the ground echoed through the alley.

"Don't move!" Angus shouted, pinning the shooter down. Miguel was right behind him, his gun trained on the suspect.

The shooter struggled briefly before going still, realizing there was no escape. Angus pulled off the mask hiding the shooter's identity and revealed a young man with animosity in his eyes.

"Who sent you?" Angus demanded. "Why did you kill Holt?"

The shooter's eyes flickered with defiance.

Angus's heart sank.

"Where is she? Where did they take her?"

The shooter smirked, a cruel glint in his eyes.

Before Angus could react, the shooter reached into his pocket and pulled out a taser. With a sharp click, a surge of current pushed into Angus's body.

Angus was thrown back, landing on Miguel. The world spun around him. His ears rang; his vision blurred. He struggled to get to his feet. His body ached from the impact.

"Are you okay?" Miguel shouted, helping him to his feet but looking desperately for the shooter.

Angus nodded, but his mind struggled to process what had just happened. The shooter was gone, leaving behind a scene of chaos, destruction, and more questions to which they didn't have the answers.

ANGUS SHOOK off the lingering effects of the taser, his muscles still twitching slightly as he steadied himself against a nearby wall. The shooter had vanished into the maze of the marina, leaving nothing but unanswered questions in his wake. Miguel still scanned the area, his gun drawn, but it was clear their quarry was long gone.

"We were so close," Angus muttered under his breath, frustration boiling over.

Miguel looked at him, concern on his face. "You sure you're okay?"

"I'll be fine," Angus said, forcing himself to stand

straight. "Let's get back to Holt. Maybe he's still alive. He's our only link to Hannah right now."

They quickly retraced their steps. The chase had been intense, and they were now more desperate than ever to get answers.

The sound of the gentle lapping of water against the boats was in contrast to the racing of Angus's mind. He replayed the chase over and over, searching for any detail they might have missed. The scattered debris and the smell of saltwater filled the air as they approached the spot where Holt lay.

When they reached him, Angus's heart sank. Holt lay motionless on the ground, his face ashen. Blood pooled around him, seeping into the cracks of the concrete beneath him.

Miguel knelt beside Holt, checking for a pulse. His face was grim as he looked up at Angus.

"He's still alive, but barely."

"Call it in, Miguel! We need an ambulance now!"

"We have a critically injured man at the docks, gunshot wound to the chest. We need an ambulance, now!" Miguel commanded.

As they waited for the ambulance, Angus and Miguel did what they could to stabilize Holt. Angus pressed a cloth against the wound, trying to slow the bleeding. Holt's breathing was shallow, each breath a ragged gasp.

"Hang in there, Holt," Angus urged. "We need you to tell us where Hannah is. Stay with us."

Holt's eyes flickered open for a moment, glazed with pain. He tried to speak, but only a weak groan escaped his lips. Angus leaned closer, straining to hear anything that might help.

The seconds ticked by agonizingly slow, each one marked by Holt's labored gasps.

"Holt, stay with me. You need to tell us where Hannah is," Angus urged, his voice filled with a mix of determination and fear.

"Who took her? Why?"

Holt's eyes fluttered open again, his gaze unfocused and filled with pain. He struggled to speak, his words coming out in a barely audible whisper.

"He... he took her..."

Angus strained to catch every word.

"Who took her, Derek? Where is she?"

Holt's eyes flickered with a mixture of fear and resignation.

"Travis... he... he's behind it all... the casino... Steele... money... smokescreen..."

Before Holt could say more, his body convulsed, and his breaths grew shallow. Angus tightened his grip, willing Holt to stay conscious.

"Hold on, Holt. The ambulance is on its way. Just a little longer."

But the light in Holt's eyes dimmed, and with one final, shuddering breath, he was gone.

Frustration and helplessness washed over Angus. Holt

had been their best lead, and now he was dead. The pieces of the puzzle seemed to scatter further, leaving them with more questions than answers.

Miguel knelt beside Angus with a fierce expression.

"We need to get back to the station and regroup. There's clearly a lot more going on here than we initially thought."

The wail of sirens grew louder and moments later the paramedics rushed to Holt's side.

Confirming what Angus and Miguel already knew, the medics lifted Holt's dead body onto a stretcher before they wheeled him away.

AS THEY DROVE toward the station, Angus's mind was a whirlwind of thoughts. The mention of Travis, and what he could have sworn was the mention of Duncan Steele's name, hinted at a deep conspiracy. One it seemed Hannah was determined to uncover. He wondered how much she already knew and if that was why they took her. Or if they took her to stop her from finding out the truth.

One thing he knew for certain was that they had to dig deeper, uncover the truth, and find Hannah before it was too late.

# CHAPTER TWENTY

B ack at the station, the mood was somber. The pressure of the case and what was at stake hung heavy as Angus and Miguel entered the briefing room.

The deputies looked up as Angus and Miguel entered the room, sensing the urgency that followed them.

"Listen up," Angus began, his voice commanding attention. "I want every stone turned to find out who's behind Hannah Jackson's disappearance. And I want to bring her home safely."

He took up position in front of the investigation board, moving around photos, circling key facts, and filling in blanks before he turned to face the team.

"Holt is dead. Shot by a skilled sniper who managed to get away. I don't believe he had a hand in Miss Jackson's disappearance but is merely a hired gunman to stop Holt from talking. What we do know, however, is that whoever is behind the shooting will stop at nothing to cover his tracks. He's not afraid to kill to keep his secrets so watch your backs. Now, we did manage to extract some information from Holt before he died. He mentioned something about Travis and the casino being involved in something bigger. What he meant is unclear at this stage, but we need to dig deeper into The Grande Casino's operations. We've all heard the rumors so we need to look for anything that ties Jack Travis and Duncan Steele to illegal activities. I need more than the backstreet poker games Travis has been running across town. If there's something illegal going on at that casino I want to find it. Leave nothing to chance."

He paused and assessed the room, making certain he still had everyone's attention before he continued.

"One final thing team - treat every detail of this investigation as highly confidential. Not a word to anyone. And I mean *anyone*. Not your spouses or your parents, no one! You pledged allegiance to serve this country and the people of Weyport. If you're in Duncan Steele or Jack Travis's pockets, I'll find you, and trust me, you won't want to face the consequences. Understood?"

He waited as one by one the deputies acknowledged his instructions with silent nods before they dispersed, each taking on specific tasks to gather more information.

Angus turned to Miguel.

"Let's start by looking into Travis's known associates.

132

Anyone who might have a reason to protect him by taking out Holt."

Miguel nodded, pulling up a list of names on his laptop.

"There are a few we should keep an eye on. People with ties to the casino and known criminal backgrounds but nothing that points a finger to Travis or Steele."

"We're going to need to dig deeper into Duncan Steele's background, Miguel. Go all the way back to his childhood if you have to. A guy like him didn't build his fortune on honest work. There's got to be something that ties him to Hannah's disappearance."

"What if he's unaware of it, Sheriff? What if Jack Travis is our guy and acting alone? So far, all the clues point to him being involved in this. We should just bring him in and get him to confess."

"Find me something that's not coincidental or hearsay and I'll cuff him myself."

AS THE DAY turned into night, the tension in the station grew. Every lead they followed seemed to trigger more questions and lead to more dead ends. Angus knew they were running out of time. Hannah's life depended on them finding the truth.

Hours later, Angus leaned back in his chair, rubbing his tired eyes. He hadn't slept in days and this case was bringing out the worst in him. Qualities he didn't like about himself. As he replayed his conduct throughout the investigation, he felt God's gentle nudging to turn to Him instead. And in the stillness of his heart, Angus thanked God for keeping them alive. As he turned to his heavenly source for insight in finding Hannah alive and well, Miguel entered his office.

"You okay, Sheriff?" Miguel inquired when he saw the intense look on Angus's face.

"I will be once we find Hannah Jackson alive. This is bigger than we thought, Miguel. We're dealing with organized crime, and they're willing to do whatever it takes to protect whatever they're hiding. It's very clear she was onto them."

Miguel nodded in agreement.

"Travis is behind this. I know it. We need to find concrete evidence that links him to all of this. Without it, we can't bring him down. Once we have him, we get him to turn on Duncan Steele. Even if we have to beg the DA to offer him a deal."

"I hear you, Miguel, but finding Hannah is our first priority above all else."

The sound of Miguel's phone broke the tense atmosphere. He answered it, his expression changing as he listened.

"Got it. We'll be right there."

He hung up and turned to Angus.

"That was forensics. They found something on the

bullet that killed Holt. It's a match for a known hitman in the area. Goes by the name of Victor 'Viper' Leone."

Angus felt a surge of hope push through his body.

Miguel pulled up the information on his laptop and turned the screen for Angus to see a photo of Viper.

"Look familiar?" Miguel asked, having instantly recognized the man's face.

"That's our sniper," Angus confirmed. "Let's pay Viper a visit and find out who hired him."

They geared up, the number and weight of their weapons a vivid reminder of the danger they were about to walk into, danger Angus had encountered mere hours before.

As they drove toward Viper's last known location, Angus had a profound feeling that they were getting closer to uncovering the truth.

Each step brought them closer to a confrontation with the forces behind The Grande Casino and Hannah's vanishing, and they had to be ready for whatever came next.

THE ADDRESS LED them to a seedy part of town, a place where the shadows seemed to have a life of their own. The building was an old warehouse, its windows broken and walls covered in graffiti. Angus and Miguel approached cautiously with guns drawn.

Inside, the air smelled musty and of rotting timber. The sound of their footsteps echoed through the empty space as they searched for any sign of Viper. Suddenly, a figure darted out from the shadows, making a break for the exit.

"Stop!" Angus shouted, giving chase. Miguel followed close behind, their footsteps pounding against the concrete floor.

The chase led them through a maze of corridors, each turn heightening the tension. Angus could hear his own breathing, the adrenaline coursing through his veins. They couldn't let Viper escape. Not again. He was their best lead. Their only lead.

They burst through a door into a large open space. Viper was just ahead. He turned, a gun in his hand, and fired. The bullet whizzed past Angus, missing him by inches. Miguel returned fire, the sound deafening in the enclosed space.

Viper ducked behind a stack of crates. Angus signaled for Miguel to flank him, moving cautiously around the other side. The hairs on Angus's neck stood with anticipation, his every sense heightened.

"Give it up, Viper!" Angus shouted. "You're surrounded!"

A moment of silence, then a voice responded, filled with the same defiance as earlier.

"You'll never take me alive!"

The gunfire resumed, each shot echoing through the

warehouse. Angus moved closer, his heart pounding in his chest. He had to end this. For Hannah.

Suddenly, Viper made a break for it, dashing toward a side door. Miguel fired, hitting him in the leg. Viper went down, his gun skidding across the floor. Angus rushed over and pinned him down.

"Who hired you?" Angus demanded through clenched teeth. "Speak!"

Viper's eyes flickered with fear, but he remained silent. Miguel knelt beside him, his expression fierce.

"Talk, or it's only going to get worse for you."

Viper hesitated, then finally spoke, his voice trembling. "Travis... Jack Travis."

Angus felt a rush of relief. Finally, they had something substantial on which to bring Travis in.

With time ticking by faster than they could afford right now, Angus cuffed Viper's hands and yanked him upright. Miguel was already on the radio calling for backup.

Viper squealed as the gunshot in his thigh sent tremors of pain into his leg when Angus pushed him toward the exit. But Angus ignored his pleas, fueled by his determination to find Hannah alive.

# CHAPTER TWENTY-ONE

As Angus and Miguel drove back to the station with Viper in custody, the tension was palpable. The frown on Angus's face spoke of the strain the case was putting on him, the urgency to find Hannah intensifying with every passing moment. The sun had set, casting a dusky glow over the town of Weyport, and the shadows seemed to deepen the sense of impending danger.

The drive was silent, save for the occasional exaggerated groan of pain from Viper in the back seat.

"Spare us the theatrics, Viper. It's just a graze wound. Trust me, you're not going to die," Miguel said after another groan filled the quiet space.

"I need to go to the hospital. I'm going to bleed to death here."

Miguel glanced back at the temporary bandage that

covered Viper's wound. It showed no signs of blood seeping through.

"You'll be fine. First give us the answers we need then you get to see the doctor."

Back at the station, Angus and Miguel escorted Viper into the interrogation room. The stark, fluorescent lights cast harsh shadows on Viper's face, highlighting his pallor and the sweat beading on his forehead. Angus felt a rush of adrenaline and resolve. This was their chance to get some real answers, to put together a piece to the mystery that surrounded The Grande and, more importantly, to find Hannah.

They secured Viper to the chair, his hands cuffed to the table in front of him. Angus leaned in close, his eyes boring into Viper's.

"You're going to tell us everything," Angus said, his voice low and menacing. "Every detail you know about what Travis is up to starting with what he's done with the female reporter."

Viper's eyes flickered with a mixture of fear and defiance.

"You can't protect me," he spat. "Travis will kill me if I talk."

Angus straightened, his expression unyielding.

"You're already in deep, Viper. You're going down for at least one murder. But if you cooperate with something significant, we might put in a good word with the DA to cut you a deal. Otherwise, you're looking at a life behind bars—or worse if Travis gets hold of you."

Miguel, standing by the door, crossed his arms.

"Think about it, Viper. We already know Travis hired you to kill Holt. We know there's something big going down at The Grande Casino. You help us. We help you."

Viper hesitated, his eyes darting between Angus and Miguel. The room was silent, the tension almost unbearable. Finally, he slumped in his chair, defeat written across his face.

"All right," he muttered. "I'll talk. But you have to promise me protection. Witness protection, a new identity, everything."

Angus hesitated. "That's going to depend on what you tell us. Now, start talking."

Viper took a deep breath, wincing as the pain in his leg flared.

"I've been taking care of business for Travis for a while now. Cleaning up loose ends. That sort of thing. He's not someone you cross." He paused contemplating the risk.

"Go on," Angus prompted.

"Travis is running more than just backstreet poker games. He's in charge of everything, reports directly to Duncan Steele."

"In charge of what exactly?" Miguel asked.

"Everything that's not above board or might get Steele's hands dirty. The Grande Casino is a front for a massive money laundering operation. It's on a scale like you've never seen before. Every one of Duncan Steele's casinos across the country is dirty. All I know is that they're money laundering for some of the biggest criminal organizations in the world. Panama, Cuba, Mexico, Venezuela, you name it, he's in on it. Duncan Steele has powerful allies. Trust me. You don't want to mess with these guys."

Angus's breath caught in his throat. This was bigger than he had anticipated. Much bigger.

"And Hannah? Where does she fit into all of this?"

"Who's Hannah?" He looked genuinely confused.

"The female reporter. She's missing," Miguel filled him in.

"Right, her. She obviously got too close," Viper replied. "All I heard is that she somehow wriggled her way into his poker games and nearly made it into the Dragon Room. He found out who she was and what she was up to and that was that. Travis did what he always does - fixes problems to protect Duncan Steele. And he was going to pop her that night in the alley if it wasn't for the imbecile who came riding in on his white horse. That guy's going to wish he didn't save that girl when Travis finds him."

"You know who it was then? You know who came to Hannah's rescue that night?" Angus asked.

"No clue, man. But I bet Travis will find out soon enough and then he's a goner."

"What about the woman, Hannah? What did he do

with her?" Angus pressed harder, his throat tight as he dreaded hearing Viper tell him that she was dead.

"All I know is that they found her with some hacker."

"Shadow," Miguel added to which Viper responded with a surprised look on his face before he nodded.

"Where did he take Hannah?" Angus commanded.

"How should I know? They probably have her at one of their safehouses. That's all I know, I swear. She might even be dead by now, I don't know."

Angus clenched his fists, his anger barely contained.

"Where are these safehouses?"

Viper shook his head.

"I don't know the locations, man." He winced when he moved his leg. "Look, I need a doctor. I've told you everything I know."

"You better not be lying, Viper. If we find out you're holding back—"

"I'm not!" Viper interrupted, his voice desperate. "I've told you everything I know. Please, just get me out of here before Travis finds out I talked."

Angus turned to Miguel.

"Get him medical attention and then lock him up. Make sure he's protected and get one of the deputies to take down his statement. We can't waste any more time with this guy. It's time we have a little chat with Jack Travis."

Miguel nodded and hurried from the room and returned with two deputies who escorted Viper to the infirmary. Angus sat at the table to process the new information. The toll of the past events and the investigation had tightened the muscles in his shoulders and he rubbed the back of his neck. It had been days since Hannah went missing and he had nothing but two corpses and a lot of unanswered questions to show for it. His gut churned with the anxiety of what might lay ahead. Every day that passed the hope of finding Hannah alive diminished.

He pushed the thought from his mind and willed his mind back to optimism. *Don't lose hope now. Keep going!*

Just then Miguel popped his head around the door.

"Viper's under watch in the infirmary, Sheriff. We should have his statement on file by the time we get back. I'm grabbing us coffee to go. Something tells me this is going to be a long night. Meet you out front."

Miguel's words rang in his ears long after Angus left the interrogation room and grabbed his keys and jacket from his office. He was right. Jack Travis was as slick as they came. He knew his kind all too well. He also knew from experience that the likelihood of him confessing to any of the allegations was less than zero.

His heart sank at the thought of Travis getting away with murder and in the briefest of moments, he caught himself wondering how God could ever forgive a man who was capable of committing such evil. A passage from the scriptures popped into his head.

*"Through him everyone who believes is set free of every sin."*

Angus dropped his head as he stood holding the back of his chair. God forgave every sin. Sin was sin all the same.

A faint smile curled on his lips as he worshipped God in the stillness of his heart.

When he was done, resolved to follow the facts of the case until Hannah was safely found, he set off to find Miguel and head out to The Grande in search of Jack Travis.

# CHAPTER TWENTY-TWO

Miguel glanced at Angus where they stood in front of The Grande Casino, his eyes mirroring the same resolve.

"Do you think he'll come quietly?" Miguel asked.

Angus sighed. "I doubt it. Men like Jack Travis don't scare easily. But we have enough to bring him in for questioning. Let's just hope he slips up."

Angus's mind was a whirlwind of thoughts. The connections between Travis, the illegal gambling rings, the assault on Hannah, and ordering Derek Holt's murder were pieces of the puzzle that seemed to fit together perfectly. But they needed more. They needed him to tell them where Hannah was.

The neon lights cast an eerie glow over their faces as Angus and Miguel exchanged a determined glance before stepping inside. The opulent surroundings of the casino, with its chandeliers and polished marble floors, contrasted starkly with the serious purpose of their visit.

As they walked through the casino, Angus could feel the tension in his muscles increase with every step he took. This was a critical moment in the investigation. He couldn't afford to make any mistakes. The air was thick with anticipation as they made their way to the entrance. A burly bouncer stood guard, eyeing them suspiciously.

Their eyes scanned the bustling crowd of gamblers and staff. The sounds of clinking coins, shuffling cards, and excited chatter among the rhythmic slot machines echoed through the building. When they approached the main desk, they flashed their badges.

"We're here to see Jack Travis," Angus stated firmly.

The security man hesitated, his eyes widening slightly before he picked up the phone and made a quick call. Within minutes, a security guard appeared and escorted them through a series of back hallways to Jack's office. The door opened to reveal Jack Travis sitting behind a large mahogany desk, his expression one of calculated calm. Impeccably dressed, he had an air of confidence that bordered on arrogance as he greeted them.

"Well, if it isn't the cavalry. To what do I owe this pleasure, Sheriff Reid?" Jack asked, leaning back in his chair.

Angus didn't waste any time.

"We need to bring you in for questioning, Travis," Angus said, his voice steady. "About some very serious allegations."

Jack raised an eyebrow but didn't move.

"Allegations? Really, Sheriff, you come into my place of business with allegations?"

Angus stepped closer, his gaze unwavering.

"We have reason to believe you're involved in illegal gambling operations, including those run out of the Turkish barbershop on Fifth. We also have evidence linking you to the assault on a missing reporter, Hannah Jackson, as well as the murder of a man named Shadow."

Jack's smirk faltered slightly, but he quickly recovered.

"This is absurd. I have no idea what you're talking about."

Miguel spoke up, his voice firm.

"We have witnesses and evidence, Mr. Travis. You can either come with us now and cooperate, or we can do this the hard way."

Jack leaned back in his chair, his expression turning cold.

"I see. Well, if it's official business that brings you two here, I think I'd like my lawyer present for this discussion."

Angus nodded.

"Fine. He can meet us back at the station."

"I won't be going anywhere, Sheriff. A place like this doesn't run itself." Jack lifted his chin at the security man who stood at the back of the room who promptly made the call to his lawyer.

"You're welcome to try your luck at a slot or two while we wait," he taunted.

"It's not a social visit, Travis. You're well within your rights to have legal representation, but you're coming with us now." Angus said, his face revealing that he wasn't backing down.

"Fine. But know this, Sheriff, you're making a mistake. A big one."

Ignoring the veiled threat, Angus and Miguel escorted Jack out of the casino. The ride back to the station was tense, the silence heavy with animosity. Angus knew Travis was a key player, but getting him to talk was a challenge for which he had prepared.


JACK WAS LED into an interrogation room. Within fifteen minutes, his lawyer, a slick, sharp-dressed man with a briefcase and an air of smug confidence arrived. Angus and Miguel watched through the one-way mirror as Arthur King, Travis's lawyer, adjusted his eyeglasses and took a seat beside his client to confer with him.

"I want to get this right," Miguel said, breaking the silence. "We need to connect the dots in a way that leaves no room for him to slip through the cracks."

"We will." Angus said, nodding in agreement. "We have enough to keep him here for now. Let's start with the basics and work our way up. Just keep your emotions in check, Miguel. A guy like this knows what buttons to push."

Minutes later, they entered the interrogation room,

taking seats across from Jack and his lawyer. The conflict was unmistakable, a standoff of wills about to unfold.

"All right, Sheriff, let's hear these allegations," King said smoothly.

Angus pulled out his notebook and began.

"Mr. Travis, you're under investigation for several events. First, we have evidence linking you to illegal gambling rings operating out of the Turkish barbershop."

Jack's expression remained impassive, but his lawyer interjected.

"Sheriff, my client has no involvement in any illegal gambling. If you have evidence, I'd like to see it."

Angus ignored the lawyer's interruption and continued.

"Secondly, we have reason to believe you're responsible for the assault on Hannah Jackson in the alley behind that same barbershop."

Jack's eyes flickered with a hint of annoyance.

"I've never even met Hannah Jackson."

Angus leaned forward, his gaze piercing.

"We also have evidence from the murder scene of a man known as Shadow. One of your henchmen, Derek Holt, attacked and possibly killed him."

King smirked.

"Sheriff, Derek Holt is not on Mr. Travis's payroll. Any actions he took are his responsibility alone."

Angus's patience was wearing thin.

"Which brings me to my final point. We believe you're

the front man for Duncan Steele. We have reason to believe you'll do anything to protect his business, even kill someone."

Jack finally spoke up, his voice cold and measured.

"Sheriff, I think we're done here. I have nothing to do with any of these allegations."

King nodded.

"My client is invoking his right to remain silent. If you have any charges to bring against him, do so. Otherwise, we're leaving."

Angus clenched his jaw.

"We're not going to stop until we find Hannah Jackson," Angus said, his voice hard. "And we will bring you down, Travis."

Jack leaned back, a smug smile on his face.

"Good luck with that."

Angus tapped the file on the table.

"Here's what we have so far. Sworn statements of your illegal gambling operations, your connection to the assault on Hannah Jackson, and your role in Shadow's murder. You're going down for this, Travis. It's just a matter of time."

King glanced at the file, then back at Angus.

"Sheriff, unless you have concrete evidence that directly links my client to these baseless accusations, my client won't be answering any more questions."

Miguel slammed his fist on the table, the sound echoing through the room.

"You think you're untouchable, Travis? We will find the evidence, and when we do, you're going to prison for a long time."

Jack remained silent with an unwavering smile plastered to his face. King stood, pulling his client up with him.

"We're done here, Sheriff. These allegations hold no water."

Miguel stepped forward.

"This isn't over, Travis."

Jack and his lawyer walked out of the room, leaving Angus and Miguel seething with frustration. They had come so close, yet Travis had managed to slip through their fingers.

Back in Angus's office, the two men sat in silence, the weight of their failure heavy on their shoulders.

"I'm sorry I snapped, Sheriff," Miguel said, his head in his hands. "I don't understand how slimy guys like Jack Travis always get away with these things. We know he's behind this. It has his name written all over and he knows where Hannah is. Viper said it himself. Jack Travis is a fixer, a professional at cleaning up messes." Miguel said, making air quotes with his hands. "We're missing something," he added. "There has to be a piece of the puzzle we haven't found yet."

Angus nodded, his hand stretched across his forehead with his fingers rubbing at his temples.

"We're tired and this case is taking its toll, I get it. For the record, I agree with you, Miguel. But Jack Travis will have his day, and if he is responsible for kidnapping Hannah, I'll make sure justice is served. Right now, our best course of action is to go back to basics. I have a gut feeling that Lucas holds the key to all of this. We need to find out who he is and what he knows. Hannah chased him down for a reason and we need to find out what that reason is. He might be the only one who can help us find her."

Miguel stood with determination.

"I'll get a pot of fresh coffee going and order a pizza from Mo's. You're right. We can't give up on her."

# CHAPTER TWENTY-THREE

Angus and Miguel worked tirelessly through the night, poring over public records, trying to find any trace of Lucas. They sifted through old employment files, property records, and digital archives, but each search led to a dead end. The lack of progress was discouraging, but they refused to give up.

As the first light of dawn filtered through the station's windows, Angus rubbed his tired eyes, frustration gnawing at him.

"We've got nothing," he muttered, slamming a file shut. "Not a single lead on who Lucas really is."

Miguel nodded, equally weary.

"It's like he's a ghost. No past, no records. Just that fake ID."

Angus stood up, stretching his stiff muscles.

"I'm going to The Black Cat. Maybe I can get the bar owner to crack. He has to know more than he's letting on."

Miguel glanced at his watch.

"I'll head back to the casino. Maybe someone there remembers Lucas. We'll cover more ground if we split up."

Angus nodded, a renewed sense of purpose in his eyes.

"Let's do it. We're running out of time."


THE MORNING AIR was crisp as Angus approached The Black Cat. The bar was closed, but he could see the owner, Frank, setting up for the day. Angus rapped sharply on the glass door. Frank looked up, surprise flickering across his face before he came over and unlocked it.

"Sheriff, what brings you here so early?" Frank asked, his tone wary.

Angus stepped inside, his expression serious.

"We need to talk about Lucas."

Frank's eyes narrowed.

"I told you before, Sheriff, I don't get involved in my patrons' business. I told you I don't know the guy."

Angus shook his head.

"I don't think you're telling me the truth though, Frank. This is serious. We're talking about a missing person and possibly a murder. Two people have already been found dead. By withholding information, you could cost someone their life. Do you really want that on your conscience?"

Frank swallowed hard but remained silent.

Angus stepped closer, his expression unyielding, his voice lowering to a threatening whisper.

"You can either help me out, or I can make your life very difficult. How would you like an inspection that could cost you your liquor license?"

Frank hesitated, weighing his options.

"All right, all right. Lucas, you said? Yeah, he comes in here from time to time. Keeps to himself mostly. Sits in that booth over there playing cards most of the time."

"What can you tell me about him? Where does he go, who does he talk to?" Angus pressed.

Frank shrugged.

"He's a quiet guy. Drinks alone, never causes trouble. I don't know where he goes when he leaves here. I've seen him talking to a few regulars, but nothing out of the ordinary."

Angus frowned, feeling the frustration build again.

"What's his routine like? Does he come here on a specific day or at a specific time?"

"No, not really. There are times he doesn't come for a week or more."

"When was he here last?"

Frank paused to recall his memory.

"The other night when you were here." He pushed his chin out to the corner booth in the back of the bar. "You spoke with him over there."

Excitement pushed through his chest.

"The guy who sat playing cards? He said his name was Ross Mead. Showed me his driver's license and everything."

Frank snickered.

"Yeah, I don't know who this Mead fellow is but that was Lucas you spoke to. Trust me. I know my patrons."

"If you remember anything else or if he comes back here later, you need to let me know, Frank. This is serious."

Frank nodded reluctantly.

"I get it, Sheriff. I'll keep my eyes open, but I don't want any trouble that might scare away my business."

"If you stick to upholding the law around here, you should be just fine."

Angus thanked him as he left the bar and walked away.

"I knew it!" he exclaimed when he slipped in behind the wheel of his truck and turned back toward the station.

MEANWHILE, Miguel had decided to take a different approach. He headed to The Grande Casino to see if Lucas might have been a previous employee. The casino was bustling with morning preparations and employees readying themselves for another day of business.

Miguel approached a group of employees, asking them about Lucas.

"Do any of you know an employee named Lucas? He

might have worked here or might even have been around recently."

Most of them shook their heads, but one employee, a young woman named Jessica, paused.

"If anyone knows him it will be George. He's been the casino's maintenance manager for many years. You should ask him. You'll find him in his office at the back. Through those doors over there." She pointed toward a set of double doors on the other end of the casino floor.

Miguel thanked her and made his way to George's office where he found him behind his desk just as Jessica had said.

"Yeah, I remember a guy called Lucas," George said slowly when Miguel asked about him.

"He used to hang around here a while back. I don't know his last name. Kept to himself, and mostly worked with the boss."

"Jack Travis?"

George smiled.

"Jack likes to think he's the boss around here but he's not. He's a puppet just like everyone else. The real boss is Duncan Steele."

Miguel's heart skipped a beat.

"So, you're saying Lucas worked for Duncan Steele."

"Not worked *for*. Worked *with*. They were very close. Like business partners. But then suddenly one day he stormed out and I've not seen him since."

Miguel's heart raced.

"What happened to him? Why did he leave?"

George scratched his head.

"He left abruptly. No one really knows why. There were rumors, though. Something about getting too close to some shady dealings."

Miguel leaned in.

"What kind of shady dealings?"

George hesitated, looking around nervously.

"I don't know for sure, but there were whispers about him poking around where he shouldn't have. If I were you, I'd investigate it carefully. Whatever he found out must have been serious. The boss had the door access passwords changed and everything."

"And when exactly was this?"

"Oh, my mind isn't what it used to be, Officer, but if memory serves me right, it was about fifteen years ago or so."

Miguel's heart was pounding so hard he thought it would go into cardiac arrest.

"Do you think you'd recognize him if I showed you a picture?" Miguel asked, his fingers already tapping away on his cellphone.

"I can try," George said, as he tilted his head sideways when Miguel showed him a copy of the real Ross Mead's photo.

"Yeah, that's not him," George quickly responded.

"You're sure?"

"Absolutely. There's a small resemblance but I'm very certain."

Miguel thanked George and quickly made his way back to his vehicle. He called Angus, updating him on the new lead as he started his engine.

"Nice work, Miguel. That confirms what I just found out at The Black Cat. It was definitely Lucas we spoke to the other night. Frank, the bar owner confirmed it."

"I knew it!" Miguel said. "Do you want me to stake out the bar in case he goes back?" he asked.

"It's our only option, Miguel. And while you do that, I'm going to keep an eye on Travis. I have a sneaky suspicion he might feel the need to move Hannah now that he knows we're on to him."

As they ended the call, Angus felt optimistic that they were getting closer to uncovering the truth about Lucas and Travis and, hopefully, finding Hannah. The pieces were finally starting to come together, but he had a gut feeling that the danger was far from over.

# CHAPTER TWENTY-FOUR

Angus sat in an unmarked car, parked in a discreet spot across the street from the casino. The neon lights of the gambling house flickered in the early evening, casting a garish glow that seemed to promise excitement and fortune. For Angus, the lights only intensified the tension coiling in his gut. Watching Jack Travis and finding Hannah alive and well consumed his thoughts. People like Travis always slipped up. He thought he was far too smart to get caught, but pride always came before a fall. He'd seen it happen many times before and catching Travis in the act was just a matter of timing.

The street was relatively quiet, with only a few people wandering in and out of the casino. Angus had a clear view of the front entrance, the side alley, and a section of the back loading dock. His eyes scanned every detail, noting the comings and goings of patrons and staff. His instincts were on high alert, every nerve attuned to any sign of Jack Travis.

He was anxious and adjusted the rearview mirror for the umpteenth time, ensuring he had a good line of sight while remaining hidden in the shadows. He kept his eyes trained on the entrance, mentally going through possible routes Travis could take. He knew Travis would be cautious, especially after their confrontation the day before. But caution didn't mean immobility, and if Travis was indeed planning to move Hannah, Angus was determined to be one step ahead.

Angus checked his watch. The nightlife crowd would soon begin to filter in, providing a perfect cover for any covert operation Travis might be planning. He adjusted the angle of his rearview mirror to keep an eye on the alleyways and side entrances instead, making a mental note to stop fidgeting with it. Stakeouts required patience and vigilance, traits with which he was well experienced. He rolled his tight shoulder back and relaxed into the seat, preparing for the long night that lay ahead.

HOURS PASSED with little activity and Angus sipped from the drive-thru cup he got hours earlier. The coffee was now cold but still served its purpose to keep him alert. He glanced at the casino entrance periodically, noting the faces of regular patrons and the occasional newcomer as he took another sip. Just as he was beginning to feel the strain of inactivity, he spotted a familiar figure emerging from the casino's back entrance.

It was Jack Travis, flanked by two of his burly security guards. They were engaged in a hushed conversation, the seriousness of their expressions evident even from a distance. Angus's heart rate quickened as he watched them. Travis looked around, his eyes scanning the area before he nodded to his men and got into a shiny, sleek, black sedan parked in the alley.

Angus immediately started his car, making sure to keep a safe distance as he followed the sedan through the streets of Weyport. The vehicle took a series of seemingly random turns, a clear attempt to shake any potential tails. Years of tailing assailants kicked in, his driving smooth and controlled as he maintained visual contact without drawing attention.

The sedan eventually headed toward the industrial district, the part of town that was normally bustling with activity during the workday and now showed little activity at this time of day. Angus followed, paying attention to every detail. The car pulled up to an old warehouse, its facade weathered and forgotten. Travis and his men exited the vehicle, disappearing into the building.

Angus parked a safe distance away, making sure to stay hidden. He grabbed his night vision binoculars to get a better look. There were no visible signs of security, but he knew better than to assume the place was unguarded. He needed to get closer.

Using the cover of darkness, Angus moved stealthily toward the warehouse. The area was strangely quiet, the silence broken only by the distant hum of the city. He crept along the side of the building, searching for a vantage point. A small, grimy window provided a narrow view into the interior.

Angus peered inside, and his breath caught at the sight. Travis was in a heated discussion with a group of men. He could see papers spread out on a table, a map of Weyport prominently displayed. It was clear they were planning something big. Angus's eyes scanned the room, looking for any signs of Hannah, but she was nowhere in sight.

He needed to gather more information. Carefully, he moved toward the rear of the building, hoping to find a way inside without alerting the occupants. A rusty door offered an opportunity. Angus jimmied the lock with practiced ease, slipped inside, and kept to the shadows.

The interior of the warehouse was a maze of crates and machinery, providing ample cover as he moved closer to the area where Travis and his men were gathered. He could hear snippets of their conversation, catching words like "shipment," "transfer," and "schedule."

Angus edged closer, trying to get a better vantage point. His foot brushed against a loose piece of metal and the sound reverberated through the silent warehouse. He froze. His heart pounded and his hands were sweaty. One of the men glanced around, suspicion etched on his face. Angus held his breath, praying he wouldn't be discovered.

After a tense pause, the man turned back to the group, apparently dismissing the noise as nothing more than the old building settling. Angus breathed a silent sigh of relief and continued to listen. They were discussing logistics, timing, and most importantly, the movement of a "package." He was certain this had to be related to Hannah.

Suddenly, the conversation shifted, and Travis's voice became clearer.

"We need to move her tonight. The heat is getting too close. Make sure everything is ready. No mistakes."

This was it. They were planning to move Hannah, and he had to act fast. He slipped back the way he had come, making his way out of the warehouse without being detected. Once outside, he hurried to his car, his fingers trembling as he dialed Miguel's number.

"Miguel, it's going down. They're planning to move her tonight. We need backup, and we need to move now. I'm at a warehouse. I'm sending you my location."

Miguel's voice was tense but ready.

"Copy that. I'm on my way."

Angus ended the call, his eyes fixed on the warehouse. He knew the next few hours would be crucial. They had a chance to rescue Hannah, but it would require precision and courage. As he waited for Miguel and the backup team, Angus steeled himself for the confrontation ahead.

The shadows of the evils lurking in the industrial district seemed to close in around him, but Angus stood firm, his resolve unshakable. Tonight, they would bring Travis down and find Hannah. The night was far from over, and the real battle was just beginning.

# CHAPTER TWENTY-FIVE

A s he sat in his car and watched the warehouse from a safe distance, his heart pounded hard against his ribcage and left a hollow feeling behind in the pit of his stomach. He glanced at his phone, waiting for Miguel to arrive with backup. Minutes felt like hours, and the sinking feeling in his gut told him something wasn't right.

The door to the warehouse opened, and Angus straightened upright in his seat. His eyes narrowed as he saw Jack Travis and his men emerging. But instead of moving together, they split up, with Travis heading toward a different vehicle. Angus craned his neck in search of Hannah. But it was too dark and too far to see clearly. He was at a crossroads and had to be quick with his decision - follow Travis or follow his men. Angus chose to follow the men, deducing that Travis wasn't the type of scoundrel who got his hands dirty. He started his car and maintained a safe distance as he tailed them.

The men headed toward the docks, weaving through the dimly lit streets with purpose. Angus's suspicion grew stronger. An abandoned fishmonger's shack loomed ahead, its dilapidated structure barely visible in the darkness. The men pulled up, pausing once they got out of the car to survey the area.

Angus parked his car at a discreet distance and approached the shack on foot, his heart pounding like a drum in his chest.

He waited for the right moment and then, as the men stepped inside, he made his move.

"Stop! Weyport Sheriff's Department!" Angus shouted, his gun drawn.

The men turned, surprise flashing across their faces. Angus quickly scanned the room, his eyes searching for any sign of Hannah. But Hannah was nowhere to be seen.

What he found instead were the men's amused faces staring back at him. Realization hit him like a ton of bricks. Travis had known he was being followed and had planned the perfect decoy.

And he fell for it.

Disappointment sat shallow in his gut as Angus scanned the shadowy corners of the old fishmonger's shack.

"Looking for something, Sheriff," one of the men sneered, his voice dripping with mockery.

"Where is she?" Angus demanded, his voice edged with desperation. "Tell me where Hannah Jackson is!"

The men exchanged glances, their demeanor turning hostile. Angus saw the shift in their attitudes, and he knew they weren't going to back down easily. He shot up a silent prayer that Miguel would get there soon but held firm his courage.

"Last chance. Surrender now and tell me where she is!" Angus ordered.

He prayed for God to protect him, to help him find Hannah, to keep these men's emotions at bay. His pulse quickened and he sought to maintain control of the situation.

When the men didn't answer him, he reached for his phone to check on Miguel. The exasperated look on the men's faces told him they had no intention of surrendering. Before he could make the call, they lunged, their movements swift and coordinated.

Angus fought back, his combat training kicking in as he tried to subdue them. The confined space of the shack made the fight even more intense, every sound amplified by the wooden walls.

Angus managed to land a few blows, but the numbers were against him. After a series of blows to his stomach, one of the men swung a piece of timber, catching Angus off guard and knocking him to the ground. Pain shot through his body as he hit the floor. His vision momentarily blurred. The breath was knocked out of him.

The men didn't waste any time. They bolted out of the shack, leaving Angus struggling to regain his footing. By the time he managed to get up and out the door, they were gone, having disappeared into the shadows of the docks.

Angus staggered, spitting a ball of bloodstained saliva onto the dirt. He had been so close, yet now it felt like he'd failed Hannah once again.

He reached for his phone, and dialed Miguel with shaky hands.

"Miguel, it was a decoy," Angus said, pain lacing his voice. "Travis must have known we were onto him. I followed his men to the docks. I thought this was where they were keeping Hannah, but she's not here."

"You sound hurt. You okay?" Miguel inquired.

"I took a beating, but I'll live."

"I'm turning the car around."

"There's no point. They got away, and Travis's trail has long since gone cold. I can't even begin to guess into what hole he's crawled. There's nothing more we can do tonight. They know we're onto them, so they won't take any chances tonight."

"At least we know she's still alive and that they've got her. We have four hours till sunrise. I'll get a search warrant first thing," Miguel replied.

"Sounds good. We should get some rest. It's been a tough couple of days and I'm not thinking straight. The last thing we need is for me to make more stupid mistakes. Besides, I need to get some ice on these ribs of mine."

Angus ended the call, his mind working out what their next move could be. He knew he couldn't afford to waste any more time. Travis had the upper hand for now, but Angus remained steadfast in his commitment to bring him down and save Hannah.

As Angus drove home, his mind replayed the events of past few days. He couldn't shake the feeling that they were missing something. He hadn't actually seen them move Hannah. Why would Travis keep her alive if he had her? For what purpose? If she threatened to expose him and whatever illegal activity was going on at The Grande, surely he would have killed her already. What if Travis didn't really have her?

The questions swirled in his head and he rubbed at the tension headache that originated at the back of his neck. He'd seen the look on Travis's face. Like he knew something. Was it possible he was toying with them? Intentionally sabotaging their investigation? He certainly was the type of man who'd go above and beyond to make a fool of others.

Angus pulled his car into his drive and put it into park. Exhaustion was starting to catch up with him, but he pushed it aside. There would be time for rest later, once Hannah was safe. Before he knew it, he threw the car into reverse and turned it back toward the station.

. . .

WHEN HE ARRIVED at the station, he found Miguel, poring over a map of Weyport.

"It seems I'm not the only one who couldn't sleep," Miguel joked.

"Let's hope we don't regret it tomorrow. Wanna fill me in on what you're doing?" Angus asked as he poured himself a hot cup of coffee from the fresh pot Miguel had just brewed.

"I'm marking out potential locations where Travis might be hiding Hannah. It seems he has a thing for warehouses, so the industrial district seems like a good lead."

"We should also check out the docks again," Angus said. "And let's get search warrants for both his home and his office at The Grande. I'm not taking his arrogance for granted," he instructed Miguel.

They spent the next few hours strategizing their next move, marking potential locations where Travis might be hiding Hannah. They knew the industrial district was a good lead, but searching his home seemed like the obvious place to start.

As dawn broke, casting a pale light over the station, Angus felt a renewed sense of determination. When the search warrants to search Jack Travis's home and his office at The Grande came in less than an hour after the world opened for business, there was no stopping them.

# CHAPTER TWENTY-SIX

Angus gathered his team of deputies at the station, a sense of purpose filling the air. He was more convinced by the minute that Jack Travis was smart enough to do the last thing someone would expect him to do and that was to hide Hannah in plain sight. His home would be the last place people would come looking for her. The possibility of finding Hannah Jackson there fueled his resolve. As he briefed the team, Angus sensed that time was slipping through their fingers. So much time had already been wasted on retracing Hannah's steps which only led nowhere.

"Listen up, everyone," Angus began, his voice steady but intense. "We have a search warrant for Jack Travis's home. This might be our best chance to find Hannah. We go in with caution but with expediency. No stone unturned, and no room unchecked. Let's bring her home."

Miguel added, "Stay sharp. Travis is dangerous, and we have to assume he's got people protecting him. Watch each other's backs and follow protocol."

The team nodded, their expressions stony and focused. They piled into their vehicles. The convoy of police cars cut through the early morning mist as they headed toward the recently completed affluent Lakeview community where Travis's home was located.

The drive felt interminable, each minute stretching into eternity. Angus silently prayed for Hannah's safety, clinging to the hope that they would find her alive, begging God for a positive outcome.

As they approached Travis's mansion, the grandeur of the place was completely at odds with the malevolence of what might lurk within and with its owner. The team spread out, surrounding the property, while Angus and Miguel led the charge to the front door. Angus pounded on the door, his fist echoing through the silent morning.

"Jack Travis! Weyport Sheriff's Department! Open up!"

There was no response. With a nod from Angus, one of the deputies kicked in the door. They moved inside, weapons drawn. The interior opulence of the mansion contrasted sharply with their mission.

"Clear every room," Angus ordered. "Basements, attics, closets, everything."

They fanned out, systematically searching every corner of the house. Angus and Miguel moved through the main floor, their flashlights illuminating the darkest corners. The rooms were immaculately decorated, but devoid of life. Every step they took seemed to amplify the silence, heightening the sense of dread.

After an exhaustive search of the main floor, they regrouped at the entrance to the basement. The heavy door creaked open, revealing a set of stairs descending into darkness. Angus led the way, his flashlight revealing a labyrinth of storage rooms and a wine cellar.

"Check every room," he said, his voice barely above a whisper.

They moved methodically, opening doors, peering into dark corners, hoping against hope to find Hannah. But room after room turned up empty. Angus's frustration mounted with each disappointment as he clung to his belief that God was in control no matter the outcome.

Finally, they reached the last room. The door was locked, but a swift kick from Miguel sent it flying open. They rushed in, their flashlights dancing across the walls. But the room was empty, save for a few old boxes and unused furniture.

"She's not here," Miguel said, his voice heavy with defeat.

Angus clenched his fists, fighting the urge to let it get him down. He had been so sure, so hopeful. He took a deep breath, trying to steady himself.

"Let's move our search to The Grande," he said.

The drive to The Grande Casino was somber. The

failure to find Hannah weighed heavily on them all, but Angus refused to give in to despair. As they pulled up to the casino, the neon lights were still flashing, a garish reminder of the opulence that hid the corruption within.

They entered the casino, flashing their badges and demanding access to Travis's office. The staff, intimidated by the presence of so many officers, quickly complied. Angus and Miguel led the way, their determination renewed.

Travis's office was a stark contrast to the bustling cleaning crews on the casino floor. It was quiet, meticulously organized, and reeked of Travis's arrogance and cheap cologne. They began their search, going through drawers, cabinets, and files. But just like his home, the office turned up nothing that would lead them to Hannah.

"There's nothing here either," Miguel said, frustration evident in his voice. "No sign of Travis, and no clue about Hannah."

Angus nodded. They were running out of options, but they couldn't give up. He grabbed his radio and called in an APB on Jack Travis, instructing all available units to be on the lookout.

"We're missing something," Angus muttered, more to himself than anyone else. "Think, Angus. Where would he go?"

As they exited the casino, a call came over the radio. It was a deputy stationed at the docks.

"Sheriff, we found something. You need to get down here."

Angus's heart skipped a beat. He and Miguel rushed to their car and sped toward the docks, hope and dread warring within him. The prospect of finding Hannah's body under a tarp or in a deserted fishmonger's shack gnawed at his insides.

His hunch wasn't far off. The scene that greeted them was demoralizing. Deputies were gathered around a sleek black sedan, the trunk open.

Angus nervously approached. The sight that met his eyes was worse than anything he had imagined. Jack Travis's lifeless body was stuffed into the trunk, his face a mask of terror.

"Houston, we have a problem," Miguel whispered, his hand covering his mouth in shock.

Angus took a deep breath, trying to steady his nerves and regain his composure.

"Secure the scene," he said, his voice calm but authoritative. "Get forensics down here ASAP, and make sure no one contaminates the area. Something else is going on here and we need to get to the bottom of this fast."

Miguel nodded, already on his radio, calling in the necessary units. Angus stared at Travis's body, trying to comprehend how all the pieces of the puzzle fit together. The stakes had just been raised, and his entire investigation was turned on its head.

As the deputies began their work, Angus walked to the

edge of the dock, staring out at the dark, choppy waters. He felt a mix of anger and helplessness. Hannah was still out there, and now their best lead was dead. He clenched his fists, vowing that he would not rest until she was found.

At the sound of footsteps approaching, he turned to see Miguel standing beside him.

"What now, Sheriff?"

"We go back to the drawing board and keep going. We find out who killed Travis, and we find Hannah. This fight isn't over."

But as Miguel turned and walked away, Angus couldn't help but feel a deep sense of panic. The murder of Jack Travis was a game changer, adding a new layer of complexity to the case. It also meant that he had been wrong, suspecting the wrong guy of Hannah's abduction.

Doubt settled in between the questions that now flooded his mind and clouded his trust in God. He had wasted valuable time chasing a lead that ended with yet another murder victim. It was a chain reaction of sinister events over which he had no control. He needed answers and he needed them fast.

But the thought that lingered at the forefront of his mind was that whoever had Hannah was even more dangerous than he had feared.

# CHAPTER TWENTY-SEVEN

Angus stood by the dock, the cold wind whipping through his hair as he waited for forensics to arrive. The scene was cordoned off, deputies milled about, and secured the perimeter. The stress that Angus felt was on full display as he stood there with clenched fists and lines on his forehead betraying the depths of his worry for Hannah. The grim discovery of Jack Travis's body had only complicated the case and raised the level of danger and Angus's frustration.

Angus watched as the medical examiner's van pulled up to the scene. The sight of Murphy stepping out of the vehicle cut through his inner turmoil and brought a small, involuntary smile to his lips. Her dark hair was tied back in a no-nonsense ponytail, and he sought a glimpse of her blue-green eyes that seemed to glint with a hint of warmth whenever she looked at him. Her presence brought a sense of peace to the storm that raged within him. It was something he desperately craved in the moment. She had become a constant calm he was starting to realize he didn't want to be without anymore. They had been working together for a while, their professional relationship marked by a mutual respect. However, denying the unspoken attraction between them was getting harder by the day.

He watched as she scanned the scene with professional detachment. But when she saw Angus, her lips curled into a warm smile.

"Hey, Sheriff," Murphy greeted as she approached him, her tone casual but warm. "Heard you've got quite the mess here," she added, her gloved hands already pulling out her equipment. "You always seem to call me to the most charming places."

Angus chuckled, trying to lighten the heavy atmosphere.

"I like to keep things interesting for you, Doc."

Murphy gave him a small, playful smile before turning serious as she approached the body of Jack Travis.

"Yeah, it's got me scratching my head. I'm glad you're here, Murph. This case has me frazzled to say the least. I feel like I'm losing my mind."

"I can tell. When was the last time you had a proper night's rest?"

Angus avoided her question and looked away.

"Just as I thought. You know you won't be able to keep this up if you don't eat and sleep, Angus."

"I know, you're right. I just can't afford to waste any more time chasing bad leads while Hannah's still out there. I was so sure Travis had her. I would have bet everything on it."

"Don't beat yourself up over it. Let's see what we have here, okay?" She squeezed his arm lightly before she turned and walked toward the body.

They stood over the open trunk, the body of Jack Travis lying inside. Murphy's eyes were clinical as she began her examination, her movements precise and practiced.

Angus watched as she worked. Despite the grim circumstances, he couldn't help but admire her focus and expertise.

"No sign of any gunshot wounds or stabbings," Murphy began, her fingers gently probing the skin around Travis's neck, her voice professional as she narrated her findings for Angus.

"But there are clear signs of strangulation. You can see the bruising around the neck and the petechial hemorrhages in the eyes. Asphyxiation is the cause of death."

Angus nodded, taking in the information.

"How long do you think he's been dead?"

Murphy consulted the thermometer and checked her watch, making quick calculations.

"Based on the lividity and rigor mortis, I'd estimate the time of death to be only a few hours ago. Maybe around 3 or 4 a.m."

Angus frowned, thinking about the timeline.

"He didn't see this coming, did he?"

Murphy shook her head.

"No signs of any struggle. At least none that I can see at first glance. No obvious defensive wounds on his hands or arms. I'm guessing it is possible he might have known his killer or was taken by surprise. Given how his body is in a fetal position, I suspect he was killed outside the car and then moved into the trunk."

Angus frowned, processing the information as he sighed and rubbed his temples. He looked around the scene, trying to make sense of it all.

"So, we're looking at someone he trusted enough to get close, someone who could overpower him without much of a fight and who was strong enough to carry and lift him into the trunk."

Murphy nodded, her expression sympathetic.

"That's what it looks like. I'll know more once I get him back to the lab, but this is a start."

Angus moved to the driver's side of the vehicle.

"There's no sign of struggle in the car."

Murphy glanced inside the sedan.

"No, it's surprisingly clean. Almost too clean."

"Thanks, Murph," Angus said, genuinely grateful. "I'll get them to process the interior of the car, especially the passenger side for fingerprints. Maybe his killer was in the car with him before this happened."

Murphy gave him a small, encouraging smile.

"You've got this. You'll get to the bottom of it, I'm sure."

As she finished her examination, Angus turned to the forensics team who stood to one side waiting for instructions.

"All right, process the interior of the car, especially the passenger side, for fingerprints. If the killer was in the car with Travis, we might get lucky."

The forensics team got to work immediately. Angus watched as they meticulously dusted for prints, each moment feeling like an eternity. After what felt like hours, one of the technicians approached him.

"We got something, Sheriff. We pulled a clear set of fingerprints from the steering wheel. We would assume they belong to the victim since this is his vehicle, but we're running them through the system as we speak. If it's a match, it confirms the victim was in the driver's seat. But we also found a single partial fingerprint on the rear of the car. It looks like the killer wiped all the other prints but missed this one."

Angus's heart quickened with the flicker of hope he had been handed.

"Did you run it through the database?"

"I'm doing that right now but so far nothing."

The technician walked toward the nearby tech station where he was processing the print.

"Good job. Let me know the moment you get a hit,"

Angus said as he stood next to him, the seconds ticking by with agonizing slowness.

The technician nodded and turned his attention back to the portable scanner.

Angus rejoined Murphy and stood to the side, watching the team work. Murphy's gaze softened as she glanced at the pensive look in Angus's eyes.

"This case is really taking its toll on you. Are you sure you're okay?"

Angus sighed, running a hand through his hair.

"I'm just worried, Murph. We've been chasing leads all over town, and we're no closer to finding Hannah. And now, with Travis dead, it's the third corpse linked to this case in a matter of days. What if Hannah..."

Murphy placed a reassuring hand on his arm.

"Don't say it. We'll find her, Angus. We just have to keep working the facts. One lead at a time. You'll find her and whoever is responsible for these murders. If anyone can solve this case, you can."

Angus looked at her, gratitude in his eyes.

"Thanks, Murph. I needed that."

She smiled softly as a flicker of affection in her eyes teased at his insides. In an instant she looked away and turned back to the task at hand as the technician walked toward them.

"Sheriff, we have the results on that single print and it's not looking good."

His words grabbed Angus's attention right away.

"The fingerprint isn't in the system. There's no match whatsoever."

Angus's shoulders dropped at the news.

"It's a partial print, right, so any chance there's an inconsistency?"

"Unlikely. We have enough reference points to get a conclusive result. Whoever did this has no criminal record and doesn't even have a driver's license. The database has no record of its bearer whatsoever."

Angus felt the frustration welling up again.

"Don't lose hope, Angus. Let me get the body to the lab. There's still a good chance the killer left his DNA behind. I have a hunch this wasn't a planned murder, which means he likely made mistakes."

Her statement brought a frown to Angus's face.

"You think this was an impromptu crime?" he repeated.

"I do. I mean, look where we are. Who kills someone at the docks with all these fishing trawlers in and out of here all through the night? There's bound to be a certain amount of risk being seen by a fisherman. And then he dumps the body in the victim's trunk and leaves the car here to be discovered hours after he committed the murder. It definitely doesn't sound like it was premeditated."

Angus scanned the area.

"You're right, Murph. We're completely out in the open here."

She smiled.

"This is why you need to get some sleep, Angus. You're not thinking straight."

His hand cupped her elbow as he leaned closer.

"Perhaps I just need to see more of you, Murph."

She blushed.

"Maybe," she said smiling softly. "But right now I have work to do so you can find Hannah before it's too late."

Flashing him one last smile, she turned and joined her team.

As they continued their investigation, Angus stood by the docks, staring out over the water. The stakes had never been higher, and the sense of urgency gnawed at him. Seeing Murphy was precisely what he had needed at the moment he needed it most. God had given him a blink of hope, a renewed boost of confidence, and that was enough to help him to stay focused.

# CHAPTER TWENTY-EIGHT

Hannah slowly opened her eyes, her vision blurry and her head pounding. The gentle swaying of the boat made her feel queasy, and the unfamiliar sounds of water lapping against the hull filled her ears. She blinked, trying to make sense of her surroundings. She was in a small, dimly lit cabin, tied to a chair. Panic surged through her as she realized she wasn't near the familiar sounds of the docks. She couldn't hear the usual cacophony of seagulls, boat engines, or the distant hum of fishmongers' chatter. Instead, there was only the quiet, rhythmic sound of the waves.

She was tired, her body aching from days of confinement and lack of proper rest. Her mouth was dry, her throat parched from the sleeping drug they shoved into her arm. She glanced around the clean boat cabin, its decor resembling that of a hotel, not the filthy, damp shack they'd kept her in before. A frown settled on her brow. Why the sudden change of environment? Why had they moved her? Panic swelled through her body and she started trembling and sweating. What if Jack Travis had sold her? Had he trafficked her and she was halfway across the Atlantic to Mexico or Columbia? She'd seen the wild look in his eyes when he had his men toss her into the back of his car. He was certainly capable of it. A mess he needed to clean up to save his reputation.

She scanned the rest of the room, suddenly fearing that she might not be alone. Her eyes landed on a plate of fresh food and a bottle of Evian water on a table next to her instead. With trembling hands bound at her wrists, she managed to reach the bottle, unscrewing the cap with difficulty. She gulped down the water greedily, the cool liquid soothing her dry throat and bringing a momentary sense of relief.

As she set the bottle down, her mind raced. How did she end up here? The last thing she remembered was being locked away in a fishmonger's shack at the docks. She had been held captive there for several days, enduring the constant threat of Jack Travis's men. She'd watch them kill Shadow. They were ruthless and Travis would stop at nothing until he got the flash drive. Every time the door had opened, her heart had pounded with fear, expecting the worst. Having that memory stick containing whatever information Shadow managed to retrieve was all that was keeping her alive. He couldn't kill her even if he wanted to. But now, she was on a boat, far from the shore, and en route to heaven only knows where. Had he found the flash drive she'd hidden in the trunk of his car? He'd have no use for her if he did. Selling her off would make her disappear without leaving her blood on his hands.

Disorientation added to her growing anxiety. Sorrow gripped her chest. What mess had she gotten herself into? More so, would she escape it alive?

She contemplated calling for help. She knew it was risky. If Jack Travis's men were still holding her, making noise might only bring trouble. But the silence was maddening, and the uncertainty of her fate gnawed at her. She decided against it, opting instead to trace back the events that led her there, hoping to find a clue.

She remembered the cold, damp shack, the smell of fish permeating the air. She had been in and out of consciousness, her body weak from dehydration and hunger. Then, she heard the unmistakable sound of Jack Travis's car pulling up outside. Her heart had raced with fear as she heard his voice, deep and menacing, talking to another man. The argument that followed had been heated, their voices growing louder and more agitated. She had strained to hear the words, trying to make sense of the exchange.

Then, a shadowy figure had entered the shack, moving toward her with purposeful strides. She had tried to back away, but her weakened state left her powerless. The last thing she remembered was the sting of a needle in her arm and the darkness closing in around her as the sedative took effect. When she woke up, she was here on the yacht, alone and confused.

Regret suddenly filled her heart as her mind wandered to Clara and her father. She wondered if they were looking for her and if they would ever find her now. If they even knew she was taken. A lonely tear rolled down her dirty cheek. She could hear Clara's voice in her head asking her if it was worth it. If chasing after her dreams was worth the price she was now paying. She'd let her ambition cloud her judgement. She'd let pride take hold of her heart just like Clara warned her would happen. Her father was also right. She should have stuck to reporting small-town news. She didn't have what it took to investigate stories of this nature.

Now it was too late. She was in far deeper than she could ever handle and there was no way out.

The turn of a key in the lock of the door startled her from her thoughts. Her heart pounded as the door creaked open, revealing a man with a hooded top obscuring his face. It was the same man from before. The shadowy figure that entered the shack and gave her the sedative. Had he stolen her from Travis?

She watched him come closer, her body tensing more with each closing step. His movements were jerky yet almost timid, apologetic. Or was it guilt his body emitted.

"You should eat. It's fresh," he said, his tone surprisingly friendly.

Something about his voice seemed familiar, but she couldn't place it.

"Who are you?" Hannah asked, her voice trembling. "Why am I here?"

The man stepped closer, his presence intimidating though she couldn't see his face.

"It doesn't matter who I am," he said, his voice low. "What matters is that you tell me what Shadow told you."

Hannah's eyes widened in shock.

"Shadow? How do you know about Shadow?"

The man lunged toward her and wrapped one hand around her wrist, making her wince.

"Answer the question."

"I don't know what you mean," she attempted to deflect.

"Liar!" His voice suddenly became angered, his grip tightening around her wrist. "You met with him. He hacked Duncan Steele's computer files. What was in them? Tell me or I'll kill you," he threatened.

"If you kill me, you'll never know," she braved, straining against the strength of his hand on her arm.

The man leaned in, his voice a low warning whisper.

"That won't fly with me, Ms. Jackson. If you don't tell me I'll kill your father, then your boss, Clara."

Fear and confusion churned within her.

"So, I'm going to ask you again. Tell me what you found. Where are the files?"

Hannah's mind worked at double the processing

speed. No one knew about her meeting with Shadow. She hadn't told anyone. Of that she was certain. The realization hit her like a punch to the gut. She stared at the man, her mind racing to piece together the puzzle.

"Lucas?" she whispered, her voice barely audible.

The man stiffened then straightened, his face still hidden by the hood. He didn't respond and Hannah could feel the hostility rolling off him.

The truth slowly dawned on Hannah.

The man who was now keeping her captive, the one demanding answers about Shadow and what he discovered, was none other than Lucas—the one person she thought she could trust.

# CHAPTER TWENTY-NINE

C onfusion settled at the forefront of Hannah's mind. Staring at Lucas's shadowed face, she couldn't hold back the questions that flooded her mind.

"Why?" she demanded, her voice gaining strength despite her fear. "Why are you doing this? Isn't this what you said you've been trying to do for years? Are we not on the same side?"

The man turned away and rushed toward the exit, then suddenly paused in the doorway.

"This was never your fight to fight. It's mine," he said, his voice filled with bitterness and hatred. "You kept sticking your nose where it didn't belong. Kept pushing and pushing for answers until you left me no choice."

"What do you want from me, Lucas?"

After a quick pause the man slowly turned around to face her. Moments later his hands moved to his head, and he finally lowered his hood, revealing his face. His eyes were filled with a mix of anger and desperation.

"I need to know what Shadow told you," he said angrily. "It's the only way to get what I want."

Hannah's mind whirled with questions. Why was Lucas involved? What did he have to do with Jack Travis and the whole mess she found herself in? She took a deep breath, trying to steady her nerves.

"What do you want, Lucas? Why is the content on those files so important to you?"

Suddenly he was next to her again. He pushed his face right in front of hers and she could see the look of fury and unpredictability in his eyes .

"Because he owes me and thanks to his greed, I can never get back what he took from me!"

He spat the words at her face, the deafening silence between them heavy with unspoken words of rage. The look in his eyes told Hannah he hadn't intended on blurting it out.

Lucas backed away quickly, pushing his hands through his hair as he stood staring out to sea through the small porthole.

"If I tell you, will you let me go?" Hannah whispered.

Lucas scoffed.

"You know I can't do that. You're a reporter. All of this will be in the papers everywhere and it would have all been for nothing. I can't let that happen, Ms. Jackson. I can't let you ruin this for me. I've waited years for this opportunity, and I'd rather die than let it slip through my fingers."

Hannah was trembling with fear. Aside from the day she met him at The Black Cat, she didn't know the first thing about him. She didn't know what he might be capable of when pushed into a corner or how far he'd take his threats.

Her mind jumped to the conversation she had over-heard between Travis and the stranger outside the shack. Realization struck. The other man's voice — it belonged to Lucas. He was the man with whom Travis had been arguing.

She swallowed down the lump that had formed in her throat. When she spoke, her voice was small and filled with fear.

"Where's Jack Travis, Lucas?"

Lucas frowned, the look in his eyes told her she'd surprised him with her question.

He turned around and slowly walked toward the door.

"I heard the two of you arguing, Lucas."

He didn't answer her. Instead, Lucas paused in the doorway, his back turned toward her as he said, "He's not your concern anymore, Ms. Jackson. One way or the other you will tell me where the files are. I don't care what it takes to get it out of you but you will tell me."

Hannah hesitated, debating how much to reveal.

"He said there was someone more powerful than Travis pulling the strings!" Hannah blurted out, stopping

Lucas from shutting the door behind him. "Someone who had connections in high places, someone who couldn't afford to let his operation be exposed."

"You're not telling me anything I don't already know, Ms. Jackson." He turned back around and moved to close the door again.

"Shadow was going to give me proof, but..."

"But what?" Lucas pressed, his body paused in the doorway once again.

"But he was killed before he could give me anything," she finished, her voice breaking. "I don't know what he found or what he did with the information, but Shadow said it was everything I needed to bring down Duncan Steele's entire operation."

As she was speaking, Lucas turned back toward her. Her words caused Lucas's face to harden even more, and his jaw started pulsing behind his cheeks. He closed the short distance between them and wrapped his big hand around her forearm. She winced in pain, the slightest of squeals escaping from her mouth.

His face was a mask of darkness, his eyes flashed with deadly threats.

"If you're lying to me, Hannah Jackson, it will be the end of you," he warned through gritted teeth.

"I'm not, I swear."

He muttered something to himself, running a hand through his hair.

Hannah watched him, her fear mingling with a flicker of hope.

"Lucas, please," she said softly. "I don't have anything. I'll let the story go. I won't write any of it!"

Lucas met her gaze, his eyes filled with a mixture of defeat and suspicion.

"I want to believe you, Hannah," he said quietly. "But trust is a luxury I can't afford right now. I need to be sure you're telling the truth."

Frustration emanated from Hannah.

"I am telling the truth! Everything I've said is true. You have to believe me."

Lucas turned away, his shoulders tense.

"I don't know what to believe anymore," he admitted, his voice barely above a whisper. "But if there's one thing I know for sure, it's that I can't trust anyone. Least of all an ambitious little reporter who'll stop at nothing to break the biggest story of her career."

Tears welled up in Hannah's eyes.

"I wasn't born yesterday, Ms. Jackson," Lucas continued, his voice growing louder and more passionate. "I know ambition all too well. It's addictive, like a drug, swallowing you whole, devouring you bit by bit like a python swallowing its prey. Once it grips you, it never lets you go. I've been there, got eaten by a snake, and was spat out like I was nothing. Lost everything because of it."

Emotion filled his words as he spoke them. Then, as if

he realized he was saying too much, he turned one final time and left the cabin, locking the door behind him.

Left alone once more, Hannah tried to process what had just happened. Lucas was right, ambition had snuck up on her and slowly but surely pulled her deeper into its grip.

As the yacht continued to bob gently on the water, the silence of the cabin made Hannah regret, fear, and doubt if she would ever make it out of there alive.

For now, all she could do was wait and hope that Lucas would come to see the truth before it was too late. The fate of her life hung in the balance of an enemy she never saw coming, and every second she was held captive was a second closer to her demise.

# CHAPTER THIRTY

The midday sun cast a golden hue over the *Weyport Herald's* office, the light filtering through the venetian blinds and creating a pattern on the worn-out carpet. Clara sat at her desk, her fingers gently tracing the edges of the scattered notes. Each paper held a fragment of Hannah's meticulous research, each scribble a testament to her determination to uncover the truth and chase her dreams. Clara's heart ached with regret. She should have seen the warning signs. She should have stopped Hannah. She should have spoken some sense into her. After all, she was once driven by ambition just like Hannah. And she had paid the price.

Worry and a deep-seated fear gnawed at her resolve as she briefly rubbed the tension at the back of her neck and dove back into perusing the papers in front of her. The office was unusually quiet, the silence punctuated only by the distant hum of traffic and the occasional rustle of papers. Her eyes scanned the notes, searching for any overlooked clue, any small detail that might be helpful to Angus in finding Hannah. The scent of old paper and ink filled her nostrils, mingling with the faint aroma of coffee from the break room. She took another sip of her cold coffee and took off her reading glasses, dropping them on a stack of papers in front of her. She'd been here all night, her eyes bloodshot from hours of reading. The cluttered workspace was in opposition to her usual orderliness. Piles of Hannah's notes surrounded her, each page a piece of a puzzle she was determined to solve. The soft hum of the newsroom was a background symphony, but Clara was lost in her thoughts, her heart heavy with worry.

Her fingers traced the edges of a photo of her and Hannah taken at the last office Christmas party. Clara's eyes welled up with unshed tears. She felt a deep connection to Hannah, a bond that transcended the professional realm. Hannah was like a daughter to her, the daughter she very nearly had but lost because she worked too hard, chased after the same dreams she saw Hannah chasing. She buried the painful memory, replacing it with memories of late-night conversations with Hannah, Hannah's laughter, and the fierce determination in her eyes. The fear that she might never see her again was a weight Clara couldn't shake and the thought of her in danger twisted Clara's insides with a mix of dread and helplessness, her mind racing with possibilities that were each more terri-fying than the last.

A soft knock on her office door jolted her back to the present. The office receptionist, Emily, stood there, holding an envelope.

"This was on my desk, Miss Matthews," Emily said timidly. "I found it when I came back from the washroom. Someone must have dropped it off while I wasn't at my desk."

Clara shook her head.

"You're the first line of defense for anyone walking into our offices, Emily. If you need to take a bathroom break, make sure someone is covering for you, got it?"

Emily gave a few quick nods.

"Sorry, it won't happen again," she blurted out then turned and fluttered back to her desk.

"Gen Z's," Clara muttered as she took the envelope and inspected it, turning it over a few times. There was no return address, no markings of any kind. Just a plain, unas-suming envelope marked with her name written in big, bold, black letters. She carefully opened it, pulling out a single sheet of paper. The message was typed in a clean, clinical font.

*"I have all the evidence you need to bury Duncan Steele and expose his entire operation. Meet me at the bridge*

*behind the God First church at midnight. No police! Come alone."*

CLARA'S BREATH caught in her throat and her hands started shaking. The simplicity of the message was chilling. She read it again, the burden of its implications sinking in. This could be the break they needed, the key to finding Hannah, and to bring down Duncan Steele at the same time. But it could also be a trap. Her mind whirled with possibilities, her heart pounding with fear and hope. The message reeked of danger. The thought of going alone filled her with a sense of foreboding, but the desperation to find Hannah far outweighed her fear.

AS THE CLOCK APPROACHED MIDNIGHT, Clara found herself standing at the edge of the bridge behind the *God First* church. The air was thick with mist, swirling around her like ghostly tendrils. She pulled her coat tighter around her, the chill seeping into her bones.

The bridge was old and weathered, its wooden planks slick with moisture that creaked under her feet as she moved across to the other side. The light from the distant streetlamp barely penetrated the darkness, enhancing the eerie atmosphere. The moonlight filtered through the trees close by, casting long shadows that danced with the wind.

The sound of the shallow, meandering stream below was a constant murmur, the water whispering secrets she couldn't quite make out. Every rustle of leaves, every snap of a twig, every distant croak of a frog made her heart leap. She strained her ears, listening for footsteps, for any sign that someone was approaching. Clara's heart beat in her ears like a drum.

Minutes turned into an hour. The solitude of the bridge spooked her, and the shadows seemed to grow longer and more menacing. She felt eyes on her, the sensation of being watched crawling up her spine. Her breaths came shallow and quick, her anxiety rising with each passing moment. The unease that had been simmering in Clara's gut now bubbled into outright paranoia. She was certain someone was there. She felt someone's eyes on her, a prickling sensation on the back of her neck. She spun around, peering into the shadows.

"Is anyone there?" she called out, her voice echoing in the stillness.

Her voice sounded small, almost swallowed by the darkness. Silence answered her, heavy and suffocating.

Clara's grip tightened around her phone, her thumb hovering over the emergency call button. She felt foolish, standing alone on this desolate bridge, yet she couldn't shake the feeling that she was being watched. She took a few cautious steps forward, her eyes scanning the tree line.

There was no answer, only the mocking silence of the

night. She took a few hesitant steps, her shoes scuffing against the worn planks of the bridge.

"Please, if you're here, show yourself!" she pleaded, her voice breaking.

Still, no one emerged from the shadows. The realization that she might be alone, that this might have been a cruel prank, began to sink in. She wrapped her arms around herself, a shiver running through her. The darkness seemed to close in on her.

Finally, she couldn't bear it any longer. With a heavy heart, she turned and walked back across the bridge, her steps echoing in the emptiness. She glanced back one last time, hoping for a glimpse of movement, a sign that she wasn't alone. But the bridge remained empty, a watchful guardian in the darkness.

## CHAPTER THIRTY-ONE

Clara sat at her desk the next morning, the exhaustion and disappointment of the previous night evident on her face. The office buzzed with its usual activity, in juxtaposition to the quiet tension that had gripped her the night before. She tried to focus on her work, but her mind kept drifting back to the bridge, to the feeling of being watched. She knew someone was there. Why did he not come forward? Was it a test, to see if she could be trusted? More importantly, did she pass it?

"You okay, Miss Matthews?" Emily asked as she approached her desk. "I made you a fresh cup of coffee. Looks like you might need it." The shy twenty-something-year-old placed a cup of coffee in front of her then nervously continued. "Are you sure you don't want me to drop all this off with Sheriff Reid? You look exhausted."

Clara frowned with annoyance at her receptionist's

subtle insult. Emily was trying hard to win back her favor, so she let it go.

"He won't know how to decipher Hannah's notes. Besides, I can't just sit here and carry on working while Hannah's still out there somewhere. She put her life on the line for this paper. I'd do the same for any of you." Clara glanced up at Emily. "Is that for me?" she asked, referring to the small package she held in her hand.

"Oh yes, I almost forgot," Emily said nervously. "It just came for you. No markings, just like the letter."

Clara's spine stiffened and she shot her scatterbrained assistant a scornful look as she held out her hand.

"Next time, lead with this rather than the coffee, okay?"

Emily nodded, her hands now folded in front of her.

"Was it left on your desk again or delivered?" Clara asked, her eyes full of hope.

"This time I was there when it came, Miss Matthews."

Clara waited for Emily to tell her more but she didn't.

"And? Spit it out, Emily! Who delivered it? What did they look like? What did they say?"

Emily's timid nature spilled into her speech and demeanor.

"It was a man, dressed in khaki pants and one of those work shirts. You know, the ones with the pockets and patches on the shoulders. I think it was like a light brown color or something."

Clara was up on her feet.

"What else, Emily? Did you see his face?"

Emily was close to tears.

"No, not really. I mean, I think he was an oldish guy, but I was on the phone, so I wasn't really paying attention, sorry." Emily spun around and ran out of the office.

Clara paid no attention to Emily's emotional huff. She was feeling much more awake now that her heart was beating too hard in her chest. She opened the package, revealing an unmarked CD. She inserted it into her computer, her hands slightly shaking. The screen flickered to life, displaying a series of files and documents. She clicked through them, her eyes widening as she realized what she was seeing.

There were financial records, transaction logs, and email correspondence. Every file was a piece of a puzzle, detailing Duncan Steele's operations. Clara's fingers flew over the keyboard as she printed out each document. This was the evidence they needed. Hannah had poured her heart and soul into this story and here was the proof she had been seeking.

As the printer spit out page after page, Clara felt a surge of hope. This was it. This was the break they needed. She gathered the papers into a folder, her resolve strengthening with each page she added.

Clara stared at the pages of documents sprawled across her desk, putting together the evidence. She needed to verify the information she had received and decided to start by checking the title deed of The Grande. Reaching for her phone, she quickly dialed the number of a trusted friend at the county office.

"Hey, Tony, it's Clara," she greeted, trying to keep her voice steady despite the hurry she felt.

"Clara! Long time no talk. What's up?" Tony replied, his voice friendly and familiar.

"I need a favor. Can you pull the original records for The Grande Casino's title deed? I need to verify something."

Tony hesitated for a moment. "Sure thing. What's going on?"

"It's a long story, Tony. But it's really important. Could you email it to me, please? It's urgent," she added, the tension evident in her tone.

"Absolutely. I'll get on it right away and send it over as soon as I have it," Tony assured her.

"Thank you, Tony. I really appreciate it," she said, relief washing over her.

"No problem. Take care," Tony replied before hanging up.

With that part of her plan in motion, Clara turned her attention back to her computer. She needed to dig deeper into Duncan Steele's background. Her mind was going a million miles an hour. As she looked up, she spotted Emily passing her office.

"Emily! Come here for a second," she yelled, stopping Emily in her tracks.

"Yes, Miss Matthews?"

"Where would you go if you want to dig up dirt on someone?"

Emily smiled and shrugged her shoulders.

"Social media?" she answered as if she was being tested.

Clara snapped her fingers and yelled, "Yes! Genius!" instantly putting a satisfied smile on Emily's face.

Opening her browser, Clara navigated to social media sites and began searching for Steele's profiles. It didn't take long to find him. His posts were carefully curated, showcasing his lavish lifestyle, business ventures, and social connections. As she scrolled through his timeline, she noted a few references to his college days.

One post in particular caught her eye—a photo of Duncan with a group of friends at a reunion event. The caption read, "Great to catch up with old friends from Coastal State University!" Clara's heart skipped a beat. She now had the name of his college.

She quickly accessed the digital database for Coastal State University, and navigated to the yearbooks section where she typed in the relevant years. The search results yielded several yearbooks, and she clicked on the one that matched the timeframe of Duncan's college years.

Flipping through the digital pages, Clara scanned for any mention of Duncan Steele. After a few minutes, she found him—a young Duncan smiling confidently in a group photo with several other students. She also spotted a name that teased her memory. Something about the name sounded familiar but she couldn't place it. Then it hit her. She printed out the yearbook pages, the printer humming as it produced the evidence she needed.

She gathered the warm pages from the printer, stacking them neatly before clasping them together with two bulldog clips. Holding the documents in her hands, Clara felt a mix of triumph and anxiety. This was another piece of the puzzle, another step closer to finding Hannah and uncovering the truth.

Sitting back down at her desk, Clara's mind buzzed with the possibilities. She had the evidence against Duncan Steele, but there was still so much to piece together. She glanced at her email, waiting for Tony's response, and took a deep breath. Every moment brought her closer to exposing the corruption that had put Hannah in danger. When Tony's email popped up in her inbox, she printed it and added it to the folder.

With the folder clutched tightly in her hands, Clara left the office, her pulse accelerating with conviction. She climbed into her car, the engine roaring to life. The road ahead was clear, the path to Angus's office lit by the morning sun. She knew that this was just the beginning, that the path to finding Hannah was still unknown. But with this evidence, they had a chance. A chance to find new leads, to bring justice to those responsible.

As she drove, her thoughts were a whirlwind of emotions. The fear and the determination mingled together, fueling her resolve. She would see this through, no matter what it took. For Hannah, for justice, for the truth.

The road stretched out before her, each mile bringing her closer to the answers so desperately needed. And as the morning light bathed the world in a golden glow, Clara felt a glimmer of hope. They were one step closer to finding Hannah, to bringing down Duncan Steele, and to uncovering the truth that had eluded them for so long.

# CHAPTER THIRTY-TWO

Angus sat in his cluttered office, his desk buried under stacks of papers, crime scene photos, and maps. The fluorescent ceiling light cast a harsh glow, highlighting the worry lines etched into his face. He had been working tirelessly, poring over every detail of the case, trying to find any clues that could lead them to Hannah. The evidence they had gathered so far painted a bleak picture, but it also left many questions unanswered.

As he leaned back in his chair, rubbing his temples in an attempt to ease the pounding headache that had been simmering for days, the door to his office burst open. Clara stormed in, her eyes blazing with determination.

"Angus, you need to see this," she said, as she slapped a thick folder onto his desk.

Angus looked up, surprised by her sudden entrance.

"Clara, what's going on? What's all this?"

"I've been doing some digging into The Grande and Duncan Steele, going over all of Hannah's notes, making a few calls, et cetera. Then this came for me yesterday." She dropped a letter on top of the desk in front of Angus before she continued. "It was delivered to the office. No return address. No signature. Just a typed letter saying he has all the evidence we need to bury Duncan Steele and expose his entire operation."

"Who does?"

"I have no idea. Aren't you listening?" she snapped, then added, "Sorry, too much coffee. He told me to meet him last night on the bridge behind the *God First* church. Here, see for yourself."

She backed away and started pacing the space in front of his desk.

Angus took a fresh pair of gloves from his desk drawer and slipped them on before he took the letter from the envelope and read it.

"Do you have any idea who might have sent this?" he asked before slipping it into an evidence bag.

"I don't but I did manage to get the evidence." Clara's eyes sparkled with triumph.

"So, you did meet him."

"Not exactly."

"What does that mean?"

"I tried to set up a meeting, like we do with all our sources, but he never arrived. Then this came in the mail this morning."

She tipped the contents of a manila envelope marked with her name on it out onto the desk, dropping an unmarked CD in front of Angus.

"Everything on this compact disc is printed out in this folder. I thought you might find it useful," she replied, pushing the thick folder towards him.

Angus opened the folder and started skimming through the documents inside. There were financial records, property deeds, and a series of emails that detailed Steele's connections to various unsavory individuals. Each piece of information was like a puzzle piece, slowly coming together to form a clearer picture of Steele's operations.

"This is incredible, Clara. But how do we know if any of this is true?" Angus asked, his voice filled with suspicion.

"Why wouldn't it be? I've been doing this long enough to know when I'm being taken for a ride, Angus. Trust me. This isn't a hoax. Whoever this is has inside track into all Duncan Steele's files. Look at the deed. I was suspicious too, so I had a friend down at the county office run a check on The Grande's title deed and it checks out. This stuff is legit. My guess is we have a whistleblower who has direct access to Steele's office."

Angus pushed the file aside.

"All this is great, Clara, but it doesn't tell us where Hannah is. All this does is prove the allegations against Duncan Steele and his casino. That he's possibly laundering money and in bed with a slew of criminals. We still don't know who took Hannah or who's responsible for the three dead bodies I have in the ME's office."

Clara's hand disappeared inside her tote bag, retrieving a book she dropped on the desk in front of Angus.

"I also brought you this." She pushed the printed pages of the college yearbook across the desk.

Angus raised an eyebrow.

"These are from a yearbook. How does this fit in?"

Clara flipped through the pages and pointed to a group photo.

"Look closely at the names."

Angus leaned in, his eyes scanning the faces and names. His heart skipped a beat when he recognized one of the names: Lucas. The same name that had been haunting their investigation.

"Lucas...It can't be," Angus muttered, his mind racing.

Clara nodded.

"The other day, when you called me in to identify the fabric, you had asked if the name Lucas meant anything to me." She prodded the picture above the name. "This guy's name is Lucas, standing next to Duncan Steele."

Angus stared at the photo, the pieces of the puzzle clicking into place to create a full picture. "You're right and this man happens to be the same guy we saw at The Black Cat the other day, except he called himself Ross Mead, which we subsequently found out belonged to a man who has been dead nearly fifteen years. He's been using a stolen identity. Since then he has vanished and we've not been able to track him down."

"Well, it turns out, he and Duncan Steele were best friends in college. They even opened several casinos together before their partnership soured. Look!" She drew his attention to an old newspaper clipping she had found in the *Herald's* archives.

Angus jumped up, excitement coursing through his tired body.

"This is huge, Clara. Thank you for bringing this to me."

She smiled, her eyes softening.

"I just want to find Hannah. Whatever it takes."

"I know. We're pulling out all the stops and with this new information, I'm certain we will find her very soon."

Angus picked up the phone and called Miguel into his office. When he arrived, Angus handed him the copies of the yearbook.

"Look at this, Miguel. Recognize anyone?" Angus said jabbing at the picture.

Miguel's eyes widened as he scanned the page.

"That's him. The guy from the bar."

Angus nodded.

"Turns out his real name *is* Lucas. Just as we suspected. He and Duncan Steele go back years. They were college friends and later business partners. This confirms the intel we got from the maintenance manager at The Grande. It explains what he said about them working together."

Miguel shook his head in disbelief.

"So, Lucas and Steele were business partners who had a falling out."

"Exactly," Angus said. "And now we know that Lucas is a lot more involved in this case than he let on. We need to dig deeper into his background. Find out where he might be hiding out."

Clara handed Angus another document from the folder.

"Here, this might help. It's a list of properties and assets owned by a shell company linked to Duncan Steele. I looked into the members of the company, but none jumped out at me until now. Guess what name it is." She smiled.

"Ross Mead."

"Bingo!" she exclaimed. "Lucas obviously used his alias. I bet Steele doesn't even know it's him."

Angus traced his finger down the list of properties and assets.

"Most of them look like ordinary places of business. A few apartment blocks, car dealerships, casinos, clean investments. Nothing that shouts hideout."

Miguel, who had been going through the papers in the folder, was crosschecking some things on Angus's computer.

"Interesting," he said. "The shell company owns a

fishing cabin by the lake as well as a luxury yacht. It could be worth checking them out."

Angus felt a renewed sense of promise.

"Agreed!" he said.

Armed with the new information Clara had provided, Angus and Miguel stood at his desk, a map of the area spread before them. Red circles marked the properties listed in the document, though their sole focus was now on the lake cabin and the yacht.

Angus traced a route on the map surrounding the lake cabin.

"It's isolated enough and not far from The Black Cat. How convenient? My guess is that this is exactly where he lives and hopefully, where he's keeping Hannah."

Miguel nodded in agreement.

"This could be it. Miguel, let's get a tactical team together. I want to be there within the hour. Have someone locate the yacht's location as a backup. We cannot afford to lose more time on this case."

"Copy that, Sheriff. I'll coordinate with the team and get everything ready," Miguel acknowledged before he hurried to assemble the team.

Angus turned to Clara.

"Thank you. You might have just given us the break we needed."

Clara smiled, a glimmer of hope in her eyes.

"Bring her home, Angus. Just bring Hannah home."

# CHAPTER THIRTY-THREE

As Miguel left to make the necessary arrangements, Angus looked deeper into Lucas and Duncan's history together. He couldn't shake the feeling that there was more to uncover about Lucas. Flipping through their college webpages, he found the section dedicated to notable alumni and their achievements. Another quick search on the Internet spat out an old newspaper article. There, in bold letters, was an entry about Duncan Steele and Lucas Clark. It detailed their early success in several start-up businesses and hinted at a mysterious falling out that led to their split.

His phone buzzed on the desk, pulling him from his thoughts. It was a text from Murphy:

*"Found something on Travis. Call me when you can."*

ANGUS DIDN'T HESITATE and dialed her number right away.

"What do you have for me, Murph? Things are really shaking up over here."

"I found alcohol and traces of Rohypnol in his stomach contents. The tox report just confirmed it. The guy was drugged. Here's the thing though; it wasn't enough to knock him out. It just caused extreme drowsiness."

"That explains why he didn't put up a fight," Angus responded.

"Exactly, and it wasn't in his system long before he died either. Just long enough for him to appear drunk. My guess is that's how the killer got him into the trunk of his car without any effort. The guy was lucid enough to move and probably thought he was being tucked into bed."

"So, he was killed in the trunk of his car. Are you sure?" Angus questioned.

"Definitely, the timelines check out, which brings me to the murder weapon. He was strangled with a rope that carries all the markings of a nautical rope, which makes sense since he was found near the docks. It was tied in a noose then removed. You will likely find hair and skin in its fibers when you find it."

"And you're certain it's a nautical rope."

"Without a doubt. I found fibers of the rope in his lesions."

"This ties in with some new information we just found, Murph, thank you."

After they hung up, Angus joined Miguel in the conference room where he was finalizing the plans with the team. Angus shared the new information with him, their fortitude growing stronger with each piece of the puzzle.

"Who's looking into the location of the yacht?" Angus asked.

"Tammy's on it," Miguel answered.

Angus walked to Tammy's desk.

"Any news on that yacht's location yet, Tammy?"

"Not quite, Sheriff. The global navigation tracking system last recorded a location about thirty miles up the coast. I've spoken to all the harbormasters north and south of Weyport, but they've not got it logged anywhere."

"What about here? Is there a chance it's in our own marina?" Angus asked.

"I've been trying to get hold of our harbor master to find out. Apparently, I just missed him. Something about him taking an early lunch today."

"Track him down, Tammy. We can't wait. Try the Lobster Shack. I've seen him there a few times. Call me the moment you know the yacht's location and have the Coast Guard on standby."

"Will do, Sheriff."

. . .

BY MID AFTERNOON, they were ready to move out. The team was assembled, armed with the latest intel and a clear objective: find Hannah and bring her home.

The convoy of police vehicles moved silently through the afternoon heat. The drive to the lake cabin was tense with anticipation. Angus and Miguel led the convoy, their eyes scanning the surroundings for any sign of movement. As they approached the property, they parked a short distance away and proceeded on foot. The dense forest provided ample cover, allowing them to move undetected. Angus held up a hand, signaling for the team to halt. He pointed to a faint trail leading toward the cabin. The isolation of the location struck Angus. It was the perfect hideaway, secluded and away from prying eyes.

They moved silently, their footsteps muffled by the thick underbrush. The cabin came into view; its weathered exterior blended seamlessly with the natural surroundings. The team spread out, surrounding the property, while Angus and Miguel led the charge to the front door. Angus pounded on the door, his fist echoing through the silent morning.

"Weyport Sheriff's Department! Open up!" Angus shouted.

There was no response. With a nod from Angus, one of the deputies kicked in the door. The team swept inside, their flashlights cutting through the dim interior. The cabin was empty save for a few pieces of old furniture and discarded supplies.

"Clear," the team called out one by one.

"She's not here," Miguel said, his voice heavy with disappointment.

Angus clenched his fists, fighting the urge to let despair take hold. They had been so hopeful. He took a deep breath, trying to steady himself and turned to the team.

"Search the perimeter," he ordered, his voice steady but strained. "She could be in an outbuilding or hidden nearby. Look for tracks, anything that might tell us they were here or where they went."

The team nodded in unison and moved outside, spreading out across the property. As the deputies fanned out, Angus and Miguel combed through the cabin, looking for clues to indicate that someone had been there recently. The two rooms were sparsely furnished and showed no signs of life. Every step they took heightened the sense of dread that they had chased down another dead lead.

Satisfied that Hannah wasn't anywhere inside the cabin, they headed toward a small shed that sat at the edge of the clearing. They approached quietly and cautiously, the silence broken only by the crunch of dried twigs under their boots.

Angus swung the door open, and Miguel shone his flashlight inside. The shed was filled with gardening tools and old equipment, but still no sign of Hannah. They searched every corner, turning over boxes and moving items aside, but the result was the same—nothing.

Frustration gnawed at Angus. They had been so sure this would be the place. He stepped outside, looking around the property for any other signs they might have missed. The afternoon light was starting to disappear through the trees, casting a creepy glow over the scene.

"Over here!" a deputy called from the edge of the property. Angus and Miguel hurried over, expectation pounding in their chests. The deputy stood near a cluster of trees, pointing to a narrow path that led deeper into the woods.

Angus nodded, and they followed the path, their flashlights revealing the thick foliage. The woods were dense, and the air was heavy with the scent of pine and damp earth. The path twisted and turned, leading them deeper into the forest.

After several minutes, they came to a small clearing. In the center of the clearing was an old, dilapidated cabin, its roof sagging and walls covered in ivy. Angus approached cautiously, his hand resting on the butt of his gun.

"Miguel, check the perimeter," Angus ordered. "I'll take a look inside."

Miguel nodded and began to circle the cabin, his flashlight sweeping the area. Angus stepped onto the creaky porch and pushed the door open. The interior was dark and musty, filled with the smell of mildew and rotting wood. Cobwebs dangled like curtains from the roof and walls, telling them it hadn't been occupied for many years.

"I'm calling it," Angus finally said, disappointment in his voice. "Round them up, Miguel. There's nothing here."

Just as Angus was about to leave, his phone buzzed in his pocket. He pulled it out and saw a number from the office on the screen. He answered quickly, hoping for new information from Tammy.

"Tammy, what do you have?" Angus asked, his voice filled with urgency.

"I have a location on the yacht. A fishing trawler spotted it about a mile off the coast. The GPS must be switched off which explains why no one was able to pick it up on the tracking system. I have the Coast Guard standing by at the marina."

"Great job, Tammy. Tell them we're on our way," Angus replied before ending the call.

He called Miguel over.

"We need to head to the marina. Tammy located the yacht."

Miguel nodded, understanding the hurry. They gathered the team and headed to the marina filled with a renewed sense of purpose.

# CHAPTER THIRTY-FOUR

The Coast Guard boat cut through the inky waters. Its motor hummed beneath the tension-filled silence of the crew. The sky had darkened; the last sliver of sunset had slipped below the horizon, casting the ocean in a shroud of twilight. Angus stood at the bow, the cool wind whipping through his hair as he scanned the horizon for the yacht. His eyes, sharp and vigilant, finally caught sight of the sleek vessel, a shadow against the dimming sky.

"We're close, get ready," he murmured to Miguel, who stood beside him, flashlight in hand, ready for whatever lay ahead.

Miguel nodded, his jaw set with determination. The team members around them readied themselves, their faces a mix of steely resolve and underlying apprehension. As the boat neared the yacht, the gentle lapping of waves against the hull became a steady rhythm, heightening the anticipation.

"Remember, silence is key," Angus whispered to the team. "We don't know what we're walking into, and we definitely don't want to let him know we're coming for him."

The Coast Guard boat slowed, its engine falling to a murmur as they approached the yacht. With only a few lights on, the vessel appeared almost ghostly in the semi-darkness. As if it intentionally tried to hide in the calm waters. They cut the motor and drifted silently the rest of the way so as to not give away their arrival. With practiced ease, the team boarded the yacht, their movements smooth and coordinated. The deck beneath their feet creaked softly, the only sound amidst the encompassing quiet.

Angus motioned for the team to spread out. They moved silently, their night vision goggles guiding the way across the polished teak of the deck. The salty scent of the sea mingled with a faint, lingering odor of diesel fuel, creating an unsettling atmosphere.

The yacht's main cabin door stood ajar, swaying slightly with the motion of the waves. Angus took point, pushing the door open with a measured hand. The hinges groaned in protest, the sound unnaturally loud in the silence. He stepped inside, two of the team members following close behind.

The interior was filled with luxurious furnishings, rich mahogany panels, and plush carpets which spoke of opulence. Yet there was an underlying tension, as if the yacht itself held its breath.

"Spread out. Check every nook and cranny starting with the cabins," Angus instructed, his voice barely more than a whisper.

Miguel and two deputies branched off, sweeping through the adjacent rooms. Angus moved deeper into the interior, his flashlight illuminating the path ahead. The air was thick, heavy with the smell of stale air and a hint of something metallic—blood, perhaps.

In the galley, a plate of half-eaten food lay abandoned on the counter, its contents congealed and cold. Angus moved past it, his focus on the main salon. The room was empty and the furnishings undisturbed. A sense of unease crept over him. He had expected to find Lucas here, guarding Hannah, but so far there was no sign of either of them.

A faint sound reached his ears, like a muffled whimper. Angus took some deep breaths to calm the pounding in his chest as he followed the sound. At a door at the end of the corridor, he motioned for the team to gather.

Angus slammed his shoulder into the door and broke it open, revealing a small cabin dimly lit by a single overhead light. The sight that met his eyes filled him with both relief and a surge of anger. Hannah sat in a chair, her wrists bound with rough rope, her face pale and drawn. She looked up, eyes widening with first fear then hope.

"Hannah," Angus breathed, rushing to her side. He

quickly untied her.

"Angus," Hannah whispered, her voice hoarse. "I can't believe you found me."

Miguel entered the cabin, his eyes scanning the room.

"No sign of Lucas?"

"None," Angus replied, his jaw tight. "He has to be here somewhere."

"So far we haven't found him but the team's still looking."

"We need to get her out of here. Now!" Angus said as soon as he untied her.

As they helped Hannah to her feet, Angus noticed something in the corner of the cabin—a rope, coiled and tied in a noose, lying on the floor. He approached it carefully, the sight of it sending a chill down his spine. It was a nautical rope, the fibers were rough, and there were faint traces of blood on it.

"This must be the rope used on Travis," Miguel said gravely.

Angus nodded, his expression hardening.

"Let's secure it as evidence. It's crucial."

With Hannah safely in their care, they moved swiftly back through the yacht. The return to the deck was fraught with tension with each creak and groan of the vessel setting their nerves on edge. The cool night air hit them as they emerged, a vivid contrast to the stifling atmosphere below deck.

The Coast Guard boat waited, its engine idling softly.

They helped Hannah aboard, her steps unsteady, but her relief evident. Angus glanced back at the yacht, frustration gnawing at him. Lucas had slipped through their fingers once again.

"We have a team on their way as we speak, Sheriff," the coast guard team leader informed him. "We'll be here waiting for him if he returns tonight."

Angus thanked him as they pulled away. The scent of saltwater was sharp in the air, mingling with the faint diesel fumes from the boat's engine. The rhythmic sound of the waves against the hull served as a reminder of the vastness of their search. Angus sat beside Hannah.

"Hannah, did Lucas say anything to you? Did he confess to murdering Travis?" Angus asked gently.

"Travis is dead?" she replied surprised at his declaration.

"He is. We found him this morning. We think Lucas killed him."

"I think he's definitely capable of murder." Her voice broke as she said it.

"Can you tell me anything that might help us find him, Hannah?"

Hannah nodded, clearly exhausted but determined.

"He wanted to know what Shadow told me. He kept asking about the files. Where they were. He's desperate, Angus. Desperate and dangerous."

"Which files?"

"Files Shadow found on Duncan Steele's computer. I

met with him and paid him to hack into Steele's main-frame. Travis caught us and one of his guys killed Shadow. A really big, tall guy. I don't know his name."

"Derek Holt. He's dead too."

Hannah's brows pulled together.

"I'm so sorry, Angus. This is all my fault. I let my ambition get the better of me."

"None of this is your fault, Hannah. You did what any great reporter would do. You're safe now."

She nodded, pulling the blanket tighter over her shoulders.

"I told Lucas I didn't have the files Shadow gave me. I lied. I hid the flash drive in the back of Jack Travis's car. In the trunk. Under the spare wheel."

Angus absorbed her words, all the parts of the investigation slowly aligning in his mind. Lucas's desperation, the rope, the stolen files—they were all connected. But the elusive figure of Lucas Clark remained a shadow, always one step ahead.

As the boat neared the shore, the lights of the marina flickering in the distance, Angus silently thanked God. They had found Hannah, alive and safe.

When they docked, Angus helped Hannah onto the pier. The team moved efficiently, securing the area and ensuring Hannah's safety. The scent of salt and seaweed mingled with the faint aroma of fresh clam chowder from a nearby café, the normalcy of it all contradicting the tension of their mission.

Miguel approached Angus, quiet determination evident in his body language and tone. "What's our next move?"

"You stay with Hannah. Make sure she's safe at the hospital. Don't let anyone near her. We don't know if Lucas is working with someone else. When he discovers Hannah's gone, there's no telling what he will do. He wants those files, and my guess is, he'll go after her. I'm going to wait for him at Hannah's apartment. Station a patrol car outside her father's house too. We can't take any chances, Miguel. I'm not letting him get away this time."

"I should come with you. Lucas is dangerous and he won't let a badge stop him," Miguel argued.

"I'll be fine. Just don't let Hannah out of your sight and call me if he shows up."

Angus watched as Miguel got into the ambulance with Hannah. Then he glanced back at the yacht, its dark silhouette against the night sky a clear reminder of the elusive figure they were chasing. As he asked God to protect them, the wind picked up, carrying the scent of the sea, and Angus saw it as a promise that God would help him face the challenges yet to come.

With Hannah safe, the immediate danger had passed, but Angus knew the real danger was still lurking. Lucas was still out there, a dangerous adversary with everything to lose. And Angus was determined to bring him to justice no matter what it took. The game was on, and Angus was ready to play.

# CHAPTER THIRTY-FIVE

Clara paced the length of her cozy, modern bungalow, her thoughts consumed with Hannah. The two-bedroom home, located not far from the *Weyport Herald* in the center of town, was usually her sanctuary. But today, the usual comfort it offered was overshadowed by anxiety. She had been waiting all afternoon for any news of Hannah's whereabouts or condition. Her phone sat on the coffee table, the screen dark and silent. The minutes ticked by with agonizing slowness. The interior of her home reflected her meticulous nature. Clean lines, minimalist décor, and a neutral color palette gave the space an air of tranquility. Yet inside she was anything but calm. The large windows in the living room allowed plenty of natural light to flood in, but today the brightness felt harsh, almost intrusive. The setting sun cast long shadows across the room, mirroring the turmoil in her mind.

Just as she was about to check her phone for the tenth time, it rang. Clara's heart leaped into her throat as she quickly answered.

"Hello?" she said, her voice trembling slightly.

"Clara, it's Angus," came the familiar voice on the other end. "We found Hannah."

Clara sank onto the couch, relief washing over her in waves. Tears welled in her eyes as she whispered a heartfelt prayer of gratitude.

"Thank God she's safe."

Angus's tone was serious as he continued.

"She's a bit dehydrated so they're keeping an eye on her in the hospital for now, but you can't visit her or tell anyone about this yet. Lucas is still out there, and until we have him behind bars, it's not safe for anyone who's been involved in this case. Not even her father, got it?"

Clara's relief was tempered by a new surge of anxiety. She nodded, even though Angus couldn't see her.

"I understand. I won't tell anyone."

"Good. We're doing everything we can to track Lucas down, but until then, we need to be cautious so keep your doors locked."

"I'll stay put," Clara promised.

They ended the call, and Clara sat in silence for a moment, processing the news. Hannah was safe, but the danger was far from over. Lucas was still at large, a menace lurking in the background who would come at them with everything he had until he got what he was after. She couldn't let her guard down, not yet.

She stood and walked to the large window that over-looked her small, well-kept garden. The vibrant flowers and neatly trimmed hedges usually brought her joy, but today they barely registered. Her mind was elsewhere, churning with thoughts of Hannah and Lucas.

She couldn't shake the feeling that she needed to do more. Hannah had risked everything to uncover the truth about The Grande and Duncan Steele's illicit operations. She had nearly lost her life for the sake of the truth. She couldn't let it end in nothing. She owed it to Hannah to see this through to the end. She couldn't let Hannah's efforts be in vain.

Determination hardened within her. Clara made up her mind. She would go to The Grande and confront Duncan Steele face to face. She had the evidence, the documents, and financial records that painted a damning picture of his criminal activities. It was time to bring him to justice and finish the job Hannah started.

Clara took a deep breath, steeling herself for what lay ahead. She grabbed her purse and keys, casting a final glance around her home. It felt strange to be leaving on such a mission, but there was no turning back now. She had a responsibility to Hannah, to the truth, and to herself.

As she stepped out of her bungalow and locked the door behind her, Clara hesitated. She replayed Angus's warning in her mind, but the decision had been made. Steele needed to be confronted. The story needed to be published, and she was the one to do it. For Hannah. She thought about Hannah, picturing her face when all this was over. She knew Hannah wouldn't want her to take unnecessary risks, but this was something that needed to be done. Steele had to be stopped, and the evidence she had found was the key to doing that. She couldn't let fear hold her back.

The road to The Grande stretched before her, both literally and metaphorically. It was a path fraught with danger, but also with the promise of justice and redemption. A smile settled onto her lips. Hannah would finally get the break she'd been after. A break she deserved now more than ever. Her own chances at New York, love, and family were long over but Hannah was only at the start of her journey. Life didn't have to end for her in Weyport.

Clara climbed into her car, the engine's roar providing a strange sense of comfort. She drove through the quiet streets, her mind focused on the task at hand. Each turn, each stoplight brought her closer to the confrontation she knew was inevitable.

The buildings of Weyport passed in a blur, their familiar shapes barely registering as Clara navigated the streets as she focused on how she would confront Steele. Courage and panic intertwined in her chest, her pulse pounding the closer she got to the casino. She was stepping into the unknown, but she was doing it for the right reasons. For Hannah. For justice. For the truth.

As The Grande came into view, Clara's resolve solidified. This was it. The moment of truth. She parked her car and took a moment to steady herself. The grandeur of the casino was imposing, but it didn't intimidate her. She had a mission, and she would see it through.

Clutching her purse tightly, Clara stepped out of the car and walked toward the entrance of The Grande. Her heart may have been frantically racing, but her steps were steady. She was ready to confront Duncan Steele, to expose his crimes and bring justice for Hannah and everyone else affected by his actions.

With each step, Clara's resolve grew stronger. She knew the risks, but she also knew the importance of what she was about to do. The truth had to come out, and she would make sure it did. As she approached the entrance, she took a deep breath, ready to face whatever lay ahead.

One thing was clear: she wouldn't back down. Not now. Not ever. She owed it to Hannah to finish what they had started, and nothing would stop her from doing just that.

The heavy doors of The Grande loomed before her, but Clara didn't hesitate. She pushed them open and stepped inside, ready to confront Duncan Steele and bring his empire crashing down.

# CHAPTER THIRTY-SIX

C lara made her way through the opulent hallways of The Grande, the over-the-top grandeur doing little to steady her nerves. Each step was purposeful. She tried to ground herself against the anxiety that threatened by holding tightly to her purse, the textured fabric giving her sense of touch something on which to focus. The walls were adorned with luxurious decorations, the sounds of slot machines and bustling patrons fading into the background as she approached the wing where she knew Duncan Steele's office was. She paused at the end of the hallway before rounding the corner and reached inside her purse to turn on the voice recorder on her cell. When she was ready, she headed straight to his office.

The receptionist at a grand oak desk gave her a cursory glance, but Clara's determined expression and swift pace left no room for questions. She pushed open the heavy double doors and stepped into the office, her eyes locking onto Duncan Steele, who sat behind an imposing mahogany desk.

"Ma'am you can't go in there!" she heard the receptionist behind her.

Steele looked up, his steely gaze meeting Clara's. He was a tall, broad-shouldered man, exuding an air of confidence and power. His eyes narrowed slightly as she approached, a faint smirk playing on his lips.

"Miss Matthews," Steele greeted her coolly, leaning back in his leather chair. "To what do I owe the pleasure?" He signaled his approval to the receptionist who quickly backed off.

Clara didn't waste any time. She placed her purse on his desk with a firm thud, meeting his gaze with unwavering determination.

"Mr. Steele, I'm here to talk about your involvement in money laundering for some of the world's most hardened criminals through your chain of casinos."

Steele's smirk widened into a chuckle.

"And here I thought you came to get the scoop on Jack Travis's untimely death."

Clara didn't back down.

"Are you denying that you're laundering money for drug cartels, Mr. Steele?" she pushed.

"Money laundering? That's quite the accusation, Miss Matthews. I would tread very carefully if I were you.

These aren't the kind of allegations you throw about in my line of business."

Clara's heart skipped several beats at his disguised threat, but her voice was steady, each word carefully measured when she responded.

"I have proof. I have documents. Financial records, transaction logs, and email correspondence that link you directly to criminal activities. It's all the evidence I need to bring you down. I just thought I'd give you the opportunity to respond before I run the story and law enforcement comes for you."

Steele's expression hardened.

"Those are some serious claims. You really should be careful with such allegations. You have no idea what you're getting yourself into."

Clara leaned forward, her eyes blazing with intensity.

"I am fully aware of what I'm getting into, Mr. Steele. And so are the authorities. The sheriff has a copy of everything. You're finished."

Steele's face paled slightly, but he quickly regained his composure.

"You're bluffing. This is nothing more than a desperate attempt to smear my name."

Clara didn't waver.

"Oh, I assure you, Mr. Steele, it's not a bluff. I've read through all the documents. They paint a clear picture of your operations. The money laundering, the connections to organized crime, the rigged slot machines—it's all there."

Steele's eyes flickered with a mix of anger and fear. He leaned forward, his voice low and menacing.

"You have no idea who you're dealing with, Miss Matthews. This isn't a game."

"Neither are ruining people's lives and breaking the law," Clara shot back. "You may have been able to hide your activities for years, but it's over now. The truth is out."

The tension in the air was thick with unspoken threats. Steele's eyes darted to her purse on his desk, then back to Clara. He opened his mouth to speak, but the sound of the door bursting open interrupted him.

Clara was stunned when she turned to see Lucas storming into the room, a gun clutched tightly in his hand. His eyes were wild, his face twisted with desperation.

"Hand over the evidence, Clara," Lucas demanded, his voice shaking. "Now."

Clara's breath caught in her throat. She glanced at Steele, who looked equally shocked. The room seemed to shrink, and the air grew colder as the gravity of the situation settled in.

"Lucas? What are *you* doing here?" Steele's voice was a mix of confusion and anger. "I thought you had taken the hint and disappeared off the face of the earth."

Lucas didn't take his eyes off Clara, his grip on the gun tightening as it swung back and forth between Clara and Duncan.

"Put the gun down, you stupid old fool," Duncan barked, inviting even more rage into Lucas's face.

"I'm no one's fool anymore Duncan, least of all yours." He turned the gun back to Clara. "Now give me the flash drive."

Clara's brows twitched with confusion.

"I said, give it to me!" Lucas yelled, lunging at her purse.

But Duncan was quicker and snatched it up first.

"You forget that I'm the one holding the gun, Duncan, so hand it over."

Clara tried backing away to safety, but Lucas stopped her.

"Please, we can talk about this," she tried reasoning with him. "I don't have your stupid flash drive. There's nothing in my purse."

Panic briefly skittered across Lucas's face before he turned the gun back toward Duncan's chest.

"Open it, slowly, or I swear I will pull this trigger," he told Duncan who immediately responded by emptying the contents of the purse on top of the desk.

"I told you. It's just my phone and a lipstick," Clara said.

"Where is it? You and Hannah are close and since she somehow escaped, common sense tells me she gave it to you. So out with it."

Clara tried to figure out what Lucas was talking about. She knew she had to stay calm, to think clearly, to try to defuse the tense situation. She took a deep breath, her eyes meeting Lucas's.

"Lucas, you don't have to do this," she said softly, trying to keep her voice steady. "I don't know anything about a flash drive. The sheriff already has the evidence. Killing me or Duncan won't change anything."

Lucas's eyes flickered with uncertainty, but he didn't lower the gun.

"It's too late, Lucas," Clara continued. "The truth is out. There's no going back."

The room was silent, the tension thick enough to cut with a knife.

"You and that silly reporter ruined everything," Lucas started. "Everything!" he yelled, his movements now erratic.

"Ruined what exactly, you fool?" Steele responded angrily. "Oh wait, let me guess. You were plotting your revenge on me. Thought you could take all this back. Well, you can't. You will never get your grimy little paws on any of my casinos. I built this! Me! You were nothing but a worker bee."

"You're a thief, Duncan Steele. A thief! My algorithms are making these wheels turn. None of this would exist were it not for my slot machines."

Clara could see the desperation in Lucas's eyes, the fear of losing everything he had worked for. She took a step forward, her hands raised slightly in a gesture of peace.

"Please, Lucas," she pleaded. "Put the gun down. Let's end this without any more violence."

Lucas's hands trembled, the gun wavering slightly. He glanced at Steele, who remained silent, his expression unreadable. The pressure of his decision hung heavy in the air, each second stretching into an eternity.

"No. If he goes down, I go down, and I won't let that happen. Destroying those files gets me back in the driver's seat and all of this becomes mine. As it should be.

Duncan bellowed a laugh.

"You really are thick, aren't you, Lucas? It's all in my name, you imbecile, and if you think I'm going to sign it over to you, you're an even bigger fool than I thought."

Lucas's face softened into a smug smile.

"It's already mine, Steele. I just need you dead."

Duncan frowned.

"He's right," Clara said. "He owns half of everything you own. He's the other fifty percent stakeholder in your shell company."

Duncan threw his head back and laughed.

"You're as dumb as he is, Miss Matthews. My partner's name is Ross Mead. I'm not an idiot, you know."

"Except the real Ross Mead is dead. He died fifteen years ago, and Lucas stole his identity."

Duncan's face dropped, his shoulders sagging in disbelief.

"You never should have cut me out of the deal, Duncan. You should have given me my share when I asked for it, but greed and pride got the better of you," Lucas hissed, his voice dripping with venom.

His face twisted with rage as he raised the gun, pointing it directly at Duncan Steele. Time appeared to come to a standstill as even the room seemed to hold its breath. The tension was so thick it was almost tangible. Clara's heart pounded in her chest, fear gripping her as she watched the scene unfold.

Duncan opened his mouth to retort, but the sound of the gunshot cut through the air like a knife. Duncan staggered back, clutching his shoulder, a look of shock and pain on his face. Blood seeped through his fingers, staining his crisp white shirt as he fell to the ground.

# CHAPTER THIRTY-SEVEN

Clara screamed, her hands flying to her mouth as she watched Duncan collapse. Lucas then turned the gun on her, his eyes wild with desperation.

"Where are the files, Clara? Tell me now, or you'll end up like him," Lucas threatened, his voice trembling with barely contained rage.

With terror almost paralyzing her, Clara realized that she had to stay calm, had to think of a way out of this. She took a deep breath, trying to steady her shaking voice.

"Lucas, please. The files are with the sheriff. I told you, killing me won't change anything," she pleaded, her eyes locking onto his, hoping to reach the part of him that was still rational.

"Liar!" Lucas roared, stepping closer, the barrel of the gun inches from her face. "Tell me where they are!"

The door burst open, slamming against the wall.

George, the maintenance manager, stood in the doorway, his eyes wide with shock. Behind him, Angus stepped into the room, his gun drawn.

"Drop the weapon, Lucas. It's over," Angus commanded, his voice calm but firm.

Lucas glanced between Clara and Angus, the gun shaking in his hand. The desperation in his eyes slowly fading with the realization that he had nowhere to go.

"Don't do it, Lucas. This isn't the way," George said softly, taking a step forward. "Please, just put the gun down."

Lucas's eyes flickered with uncertainty, his grip on the gun loosening slightly. The room was silent. Clara held her breath, praying that Lucas would see reason.

"He had no right to cut me out. I helped build all this. It was my hard work not his. I just wanted what was mine, what I took years to build. " Lucas whispered, his voice breaking.

"And you can still have a chance to explain your side. But not like this," Angus said, taking a cautious step closer.

Lucas's shoulders sagged, the fight draining out of him. He slowly lowered the gun, his hands trembling. Angus moved quickly, securing the weapon, and cuffing Lucas's hands behind his back as security rushed past to tend to Duncan.

"It's over, Lucas," Angus said softly, leading him toward the door. "None of this is worth anything in the end."

Clara's knees gave way, and she sank to the floor, the adrenaline and fear finally catching up to her. Tears streamed down her face, a mix of relief and residual terror. George rushed to her side, his expression filled with concern.

"Are you okay, Clara?" he asked, his voice gentle.

Clara looked at him, her eyes widening in recognition. The clothes he was wearing—khaki pants and a light brown work shirt—matched Emily's description perfectly. Realization dawned on her, and she grasped his arm.

"It was you," she whispered, her voice filled with awe. "You're the one who sent me the letter and the CD. You're the whistleblower."

George gave her a small, sad smile and nodded.

"I couldn't stand by and let Steele continue his operations. I had to do something. I'm just sorry I waited this long."

Clara's heart swelled with gratitude.

"Thank you, George. You saved us. You saved this town."

He nodded, his eyes glistening with unshed tears.

"We're not done yet, Clara. There's still a lot to be sorted out. But for now, let's get you somewhere safe."

Angus returned, his face showing signs of relief.

"Let's get you both out of here."

Clara nodded, allowing George to help her to her feet.

"How did you know I was here?" Clara asked Angus.

Angus smiled when he replied, "You're a reporter.

Getting to the truth is as much in your blood as it is in mine. There's no way you would have let it go once you knew Hannah was safe."

Clara smiled back.

"I'd like to see her. I need to see Hannah," she whispered.

"I think she'd like to see you too, Clara."

As they left Steele's office, the strain of the past week finally started to lift off their shoulders. With Lucas in custody and the evidence in their hands, justice was within reach, and the high-stakes drama was finally over.

CLARA AND ANGUS walked quietly into Hannah's hospital room. Hannah lay propped up on pillows, her face still pale but her eyes brightened when she saw her visitors. She smiled weakly as they approached, her voice light despite the ordeal she had just endured.

"Hey, you two," she greeted.

Clara rushed over and hugged her tightly.

"How are you feeling?" she asked tenderly.

"I'm fine thanks to the two of you and my Good Samaritan, of course. I guess I'll probably never know who he was or who lured me to the lighthouse that night. It's like a bizarre mystery novel I can't seem to finish."

Clara exchanged a glance with Angus before stepping closer to Hannah's bedside.

"Actually, Hannah, we do know who saved you from

the alley that night. In fact, he's been helping us all along," she explained gently. "It was George, the maintenance manager at The Grande. He had been secretly working to expose Duncan Steele."

Hannah's eyes widened in surprise.

"I'd love to meet him and thank him when I get out of here."

Angus added, "He was the one who sent Clara the letter and the CD with all the files. He wanted to give it to you the night he summoned you to the lighthouse. But Lucas got to you first, knocking you over the head thinking you'd back off. George risked a lot to help bring Steele down."

Hannah shook her head in amazement.

"I can't believe we did it. I owe George so much. I owe all of you so much."

Before Clara could respond, the door opened, and Hannah's father stepped into the room. His face was lined with worry and regret, but as he looked at Hannah, his eyes held a newfound tenderness none of them had seen before.

"Hey, Dad," Hannah smiled.

He walked over to Hannah's bedside, hesitating for a moment before speaking.

"Hannah," he began, his voice thick with emotion. "I thought I'd never see you again. I owe you an apology. For always making it seem like you weren't special enough, for doubting your abilities as a reporter. When you disappeared, it forced me to take a long, hard look at myself in the mirror, and I didn't like what I saw."

Hannah reached out and took her father's hand, her eyes filling with tears. "Dad, it's okay. I understand."

"No, it's not okay," he insisted, his voice breaking. "It had nothing to do with the color of your skin or the fact that you're a woman. It was about me. I was still hurting, holding on to the pain of your mother walking out on us all those years ago. But I've let it go now, Hannah. And I want to be better. I want to be the father you deserve."

Hannah's tears spilled over, and she squeezed her father's hand tightly.

"I forgive you, Dad. And I want to give you that chance."

Her father leaned down and kissed her forehead, his own tears falling freely.

"Thank you, Hannah. I promise I won't let you down."

Angus watched the heartfelt exchange in silence, his heart swelling with a mix of emotions. It was a moment of healing, a chance for new beginnings. As he stood there, witnessing the bond between father and daughter strengthen, he knew that despite the hardships and dangers, there was hope and redemption to be found.

And in that quiet hospital room, surrounded by the echoes of forgiveness and love, he felt a sense of peace, knowing that God had brought their journey full circle, and that their lives were forever changed for the better.

# CHAPTER THIRTY-EIGHT

Angus sat in his study, the glow of the desk lamp casting a soft, warm light over the scattered papers and files. The house was enveloped in a serene silence, occasionally interrupted by the gentle rustle of leaves outside. He signed the last of the report forms in the case file and glanced at the clock, realizing it was nearly 8 p.m. He had lost track of time again, but it didn't bother him. Living alone meant he had the freedom to use his time as he pleased. Still, there were moments when he wished he could share his evenings with someone special, someone who could fill the quiet with companionship and warmth.

His thoughts were interrupted by a gentle knock on the door. He stood up, slightly surprised by the late-night visitor, and walked to the door. When he opened it, he was greeted by Murphy, standing there with a warm smile and a picnic basket in her hands.

"Well, if it isn't my favorite person bringing some unexpected charm to my evening," Angus said with a playful tone, his eyes sparkling with curiosity and delight.

She stepped inside, the evening air following her into the cozy warmth of the house.

"I was in the neighborhood, and it dawned on me that you might need a little company. So, I brought you something."

Angus smiled.

"You were in the neighborhood, of course."

He closed the door behind her and led her into the living room.

"I do like a surprise visit. What's in the basket?"

Murphy placed the basket on the coffee table and opened the lid. Inside, nestled in a soft blanket, was a beautiful border collie puppy. The little dog looked up at Angus with bright, curious eyes, its tail wagging with excitement.

Angus's face lit up with surprise and elation.

"A puppy? Murph, this is incredible! I had a dog just like this back in Scotland before we left. Broke my heart to leave him behind."

He scooped him up and held him *Lion King* style above his head.

"Oh, you're a beauty, aren't you?" he asked admiring the pup.

Murphy smiled, her eyes sparkling with joy at his reaction.

"I'm so glad you like him. I picked him up from the local shelter. I thought you could use the extra company."

Angus cradled the dog in his arms. The puppy licked his face, and he laughed, the sound filling the room with warmth.

"He's perfect. Thank you, Murph."

She watched him with a tender expression.

"I'm glad. I know how much a dog can mean, especially when you're far from home."

Angus put the puppy down and went to the kitchen.

"Let me pour you a glass of wine. We can sit and talk and settle him in."

Soon they were sitting together on the couch, each holding a glass of wine. The puppy curled up on a blanket at their feet.

"I still can't believe we found Hannah and brought her home safely," Murphy said, her voice filled with relief.

Angus nodded, his expression serious.

"It's a miracle. I prayed so hard that we would find her. It's moments like these that remind me of what the Bible teaches about ambition. Unfortunately, Hannah learned it the hard way."

"Yeah, and she nearly paid for it with her life. Clara too. She should never have gone to see Duncan Steele."

"I would have rather he hadn't died, but selfish ambition, the kind that leads people like Duncan Steele astray, always ends badly. If only he knew the kind of ambition we can use for God's glory and the good of others instead.

Who knows what good he could have done in this world?"

Murphy smiled, nodding in agreement.

"Yes, James 3 does warn us against selfish ambition. It leads to disorder and every evil practice. But it also encourages us to be ambitious in the right way. Colossians 3:23 says, 'Whatever you do, work at it with all your heart, as working for the Lord, not for human masters.' When our ambition is aligned with God's will, it becomes a beautiful thing."

Angus looked at her, admiration in his eyes. He reached out and took Murphy's hand in his.

"You're right. It's about using what we have for a greater purpose. And sometimes, it's about supporting each other in those endeavors. We make a good team."

They sat in comfortable silence for a moment, the warmth of the wine and the peace of the evening settling around them. The puppy, sensing the calm, nuzzled closer to Angus's feet.

Angus turned to Murphy, his eyes softening.

"Thank you for being here, Murphy. For everything. You've been such a blessing through all of this."

She looked up at him, her eyes communicating her affection for him.

"I wouldn't want to be anywhere else."

In that quiet, intimate moment, Angus leaned in and gave Murphy a gentle kiss. It was a soft, tender kiss, filled with the promise of something more. When they pulled back, they both smiled, their eyes meeting in a shared understanding.

As the night grew deeper, they continued to talk, their conversation flowing effortlessly. The bond between them strengthened, their hearts aligning in a way that felt both natural and profound.

For Angus, it was a moment of clarity. The loneliness he had felt since his baby boy died and his marriage ended, since moving to Weyport and into the new house was instantly replaced by a sense of belonging. And as he looked at Murphy, he knew that this was just the beginning of a beautiful journey, one filled with faith, love, and shared ambition.

And in that cozy living room, with a new puppy at his feet and Murphy by his side, Angus felt a peace for which he had been longing, a peace knowing that he was exactly where he was meant to be.

*Whatever you do, work at it with all your heart, as working for the Lord, not for human masters, since you know that you will receive an inheritance from the Lord as a reward.*
*- Colossians 3:23 (NIV) -*

Angus Reid's journey continues in the 5th book, **Lilly's Vine,** where a deadly piece of gossip turns Weyport upside down!

(SNEAK A PEEK! READ ON!)

*For twelve years, librarian Lilly Cooper has been Weyport's keeper of secrets. But when she stumbles upon a diary linked to a dead woman, she uncovers a conspiracy stretching from her small coastal town to Boston's highest offices. Someone will do anything to keep the truth buried —permanently.*

## <u>ONE-CLICK TO THE URCELIA TEIXEIRA STORE</u>

**Or get it from your favorite retailer here:** https://books2read.com/LillysVine

Want updates on book 6? Join my Reader Community (newsletter.urcelia.com/signup)

THANK you for reading Hannah's Halo. I pray you were blessed with the faith message woven into the story.

**Please consider helping my mission to teach the gospel through my stories by leaving a review of Hannah's Halo. It helps others find my books!**

**TURN TO THE END OR CLICK HERE TO START READING LILLY'S VINE**

For a full and updated list of all Urcelia Teixeira books, please visit https://shop.urcelia.com/pages/reading-order

Want updates? Join my Reader Community (newsletter.urcelia.com/signup) TURN THE PAGE FOR YOUR FREE BIBLE PLAN & DISCUSSION QUESTIONS.

## MESSAGE FROM URCELIA

Dear Reader,

Thank you so much for taking the time to read *Hannah's Halo*. I would like to give all the glory to God who breathed every word through me onto these pages! (Isaiah 51:16)

I pray that God touched you in a divine way, just like He did me while I wrote it. Your support and encouragement mean the world to me and I hope that Hannah's journey has not only entertained you but also inspired you to reflect on the scriptures woven into the story.

As I continue to strive to bring faith and fiction together, I humbly ask that you help me circulate this novel by leaving a review. Just a few words or a star rating to help others find it will be great!

While you wait for Sheriff Angus Reid's next mystery to solve, I would love if you connected with me on Facebook and sign up to my newsletter where I share exclusive giveaways, sneak peeks, and release updates. Want to get to know me on a more personal note? Join my private Facebook Group. (https://www.facebook.com/groups/betweenmypages)

It has been a joy to share this story with you, and I am deeply grateful for your readership. I look forward to hearing your thoughts and hope you continue to enjoy my future works.

Warm regards in Christ,

Urcelia

PS: Turn the page to download your **FREE 30-day Bible Reading Plan** customized to the faith theme woven into this book.

For a full and updated list of all my books, please visit https://shop.urcelia.com/pages/reading-order

I invite you to deepen your journey with an **exclusive 30-day Bible Reading plan**.

Tailored to the faith messages woven into the plot, this reading plan offers daily reflections and scripture passages to enrich your spiritual life.

# free bible plan

DOWNLOADABLE | PRINTABLE

*https://BookHip.com/MTKSZNW*

Download the plan today.

# DISCUSSION QUESTIONS

(HTTPS://FREEBIES.URCELIA.COM/HANNAHS-HALO-
DISCUSSION-GUIDE)

**Initial Impressions**

1. What were your first thoughts when you started reading "Hannah's Halo"?

2. Did the opening chapter grab your attention? Why or why not?

**Characters**

1. How would you describe Hannah Jackson? What are her strengths and weaknesses?

2. Discuss the role of ambition in Hannah's life. How does it drive her actions, and what consequences does it have?

3. What are your thoughts on Jack Travis and Duncan Steele as antagonists? How do they contribute to the tension in the story?

4. How do secondary characters like Clara

Matthews and Vincent Ward add depth to the
narrative?

5. Did you guess who the Good Samaritan was?

6. What are your initial impressions of Hannah
Jackson? How does her ambition drive her actions?

7. How does the setting of Weyport contribute to
the overall mood of the novel?

8. Discuss the significance of the poker game in
Chapter 1. How does it set the tone for Hannah's
investigation?

## Themes of Faith and Ambition

1. How is James 3:16 ("For where you have envy
and selfish ambition, there you find disorder and
every evil practice.") reflected in the novel?

2. Discuss the portrayal of ambition in the book.
When does ambition become selfish, and how does
it affect the characters?

3. How does the theme of faith manifest in
Hannah's journey? Are there specific moments
where her faith influences her decisions?

4. Have you ever been in a situation where ambition blinded you?

5. Discuss the role of secondary characters like
Clara and Vincent. How do they support or
hinder Hannah's quest for truth?

## Plot and Pacing

1. Did you find the plot twists and turns engaging? Were there any moments that particularly surprised you?

2. How does the setting of Weyport contribute to the overall atmosphere of the story?

3. What did you think of the pacing? Did the story keep you on the edge of your seat?

**Conflict and Resolution**

1. What are the main conflicts in the story? How are they resolved by the end of the book?

2. Discuss the climax of the novel. Did you find it satisfying? Why or why not?

3. How do the events of the book change Hannah by the end of the story?

4. How does Hannah's relationship with her father influence her actions and decisions?

5. Discuss the sacrifices Hannah makes for her investigation. Are they justified?

6. How do the supporting characters (like Shadow and Lucas) add depth to the main plot?

**Moral and Ethical Questions**

1. What ethical dilemmas do the characters face? How do they navigate these challenges?

2. Do you think Hannah makes the right decisions throughout the book? Are there moments where you would have acted differently?

## Symbolism and Imagery

1. Discuss the significance of the title "Hannah's Halo." What does the halo symbolize in the context of the story?
2. How does Urcelia Teixeira use imagery to enhance the narrative? Are there any descriptions that stood out to you?

## Personal Reflections

1. Did any part of the story resonate with you on a personal level? How?
2. How did the book challenge or affirm your own views on faith and ambition?
3. What lessons can be learned from Hannah's experiences?

## Author's Craft

1. How would you describe Urcelia Teixeira's writing style? What are her strengths as a storyteller?
2. Discuss how the author builds suspense and maintains tension throughout the novel.

## Future Speculations

1. If there were a sequel to "Hannah's Halo," what direction do you think the story would take?
2. What unresolved questions or plotlines would you like to see explored in a future book?

## Activities

### Character Study

Choose a character from the book and write a brief character study. Discuss their motivations, development, and how they contribute to the overall story.

### Thematic Analysis

Write an essay or lead a discussion on the theme of ambition in "Hannah's Halo." Consider both the positive and negative aspects as portrayed in the novel.

### Faith Reflection

Reflect on your own experiences with faith. How does Hannah's journey compare to your own? Share your thoughts with the group.

### Creative Expression

Create a piece of art, whether it's a drawing, painting, or collage, inspired by a scene or theme from the book. Share and discuss your artwork with the group.

Download a printable guide: https://freebies. urcelia.com/Hannahs-Halo-Discussion-Guide

# SUPPORT MY MISSION

*Whatever I tell you in the dark, speak in the light; and what you hear in the ear, preach on the housetops!*
**Matthew 10:27**

This was the verse God placed on my heart the day I switched from writing secular fiction to Christian fiction. It has been my mission ever since to weave Spirit-led messages of faith and redemption into my books.

**HERE ARE FREE WAYS TO HELP ME!**
Tell a friend.
Please leave a review on your favorite book site.
Share my books on your social pages

# URCELIA TEIXEIRA

## ANGUS REID MYSTERIES - BOOK 5

# LILLY'S VINE

In the garden of faith, even a single thorn can poison the Vine.

# LILLY'S VINE

A MYSTERY THRILLER THAT BLENDS FAITH, SUSPENSE, AND REDEMPTION

ANGUS REID MYSTERIES - BOOK V

## URCELIA TEIXEIRA

AWARD WINNING AUTHOR

LILLY'S VINE

A MYSTERY THRILLER THAT BLENDS FAITH,
SUSPENSE, AND REDEMPTION

ANGUS REID MYSTERIES BOOK V

URCELIA TEIXEIRA

Copyrighted material
E-book © ISBN: 978-1-0687204-2-0
Paperback © ISBN: 978-1-0687204-3-7
Published by Purpose Bound Press
Written by Urcelia Teixeira
First edition
Urcelia Teixeira
Wiltshire, UK
https://www.urcelia.com

INSPIRED BY

"Whoever keeps his mouth and his tongue keeps himself
out of trouble."

Proverbs 21:23
(ESV)

# PROLOGUE

The bodies were just the beginning, according to the leather-bound diary that lay like a coiled serpent among the donated books. Its unmarked cover gathered dust like buried sins as Lillian Cooper's fingers trembled, lifting it from the box. Something in its weight spoke of secrets too heavy for paper alone.

The library's fluorescent lights cast harsh shadows across her desk as the autumn evening pressed against the windows, turning their reflection into mirrors that showed a woman she barely recognized anymore—gray-streaked hair pulled into a careful bun, silver leaf brooch gleaming at her collar, gold-rimmed glasses catching the artificial glare.

For twelve years, she'd been Weyport's keeper of whispered things. The librarian who knew everyone's stories, who collected confessions like others collected stamps.

Each secret carefully cataloged and preserved, currency in a lonely economy of belonging. But this diary...this was different. Its pages carried the scent of desperate truth, of things meant to stay buried.

The note tucked within its pages stopped her breath:

*They're watching. If you're reading this, they're probably watching you too. The evidence is hidden where they won't think to look—scattered among everyday things, waiting for someone who knows how to read between lines. Someone who understands the power of secrets.*
*I don't have much time. What I've uncovered goes deeper than anyone suspects. The environmental studies were just the beginning. The bodies...*

The handwriting changed there, growing jagged with urgency. Lilly's heart thundered against her ribs as she recognized the name scrawled in the margin: Holbrook Industries.

The name carried weight in Weyport—the local lumber mill and development project made them one of the region's most powerful employers, their influence casting long shadows from Boston up the New England coast like dark spires against a troubled sky. They'd brought prosperity, or so everyone said. But Lilly had noticed how the fishing boats returned half-empty these days, how the tide carried strange odors at dawn, how people who asked too many questions seemed to drift away like morning fog.

A floorboard creaked in the library's depths.

Lilly's head snapped up, years of watching others suddenly reversed. The empty aisles stretched into shadow, books standing as silent witness as footsteps echoed against polished hardwood. Not the familiar tread of a late patron or fellow staff member—these steps moved with purpose, with the careful precision of someone who didn't want to be heard.

Her fingers tightened on the diary. In all her years of collecting others' secrets, she'd never felt the weight of discovery, the cold certainty of being watched. The silver leaf brooch at her collar seemed to burn against her skin, a reminder of all the times she'd traded in whispered confidences, treating truth like a commodity to be bartered.

The footsteps drew closer. Somewhere in the stacks, a book shifted, then fell. The sound echoed like judgment through the empty library.

Lilly moved quietly, sliding the diary into her bag as training and instinct warred within her. For years she'd hoarded information, treating other people's pain as currency. Now she held something different—truth that demanded action, secrets that carried the weight of life and death.

The corner security mirror showed a shadow moving deliberately between the shelves. Tall. Male. Professional. Someone who knew how to hunt.

*If you're reading this, they're watching.*

The words of warning lingered. Her fingers brushed the brooch at her collar, a nervous habit born of years of social uncertainty. She'd spent her life collecting secrets to fill the void left by abandonment, by the mother who'd left her at St. Michael's, by the families who'd passed her by, by the man who'd left her standing alone at the altar. Each whispered confession had been another brick in her wall against pain.

But this secret...this one would either save her or destroy her.

The figure emerged from between the stacks, streetlight catching the metal in his hand.

Lilly Cooper, keeper of Weyport's secrets, stood at the crossroads of everything she'd been and everything she might become. The diary's weight bore down against her side like truth demanding to be spoken.

The time for collecting whispers was over.

The time for running was about to begin.

# CHAPTER 1

The clock on the library wall ticked with an almost accusatory rhythm as Lilly Cooper adjusted her gold-rimmed spectacles, her fingers trembling slightly against the metal frames. The emptiness of the building pressed in around her, as familiar as the ache of loneliness that had been her constant companion for the past forty-one years. At fifty-five, she had perfected the art of appearing perpetually neat and unremarkable, a skill honed through decades of trying to blend into the backgrounds of other people's lives. Her gray pencil skirt and cream cardigan were pristine, the small silver leaf brooch at her collar—the only hint of adornment she permitted herself—catching the late afternoon light.

The Weyport Public Library hummed with its usual quiet activity, though the dwindling number of patrons reminded her that closing time approached. Her carefully maintained mask of pleasant efficiency slipped slightly as she watched a young mother guide her children toward the exit, their hands full of picture books and their voices full of laughter. The sight stirred something deep within her, an echo of dreams long abandoned.

Lilly's gaze drifted to the donation cart she'd been processing that afternoon. The diary—if that's what it was —had appeared that morning, wrapped in brown paper with no indication of its donor, tucked between outdated encyclopedias and worn romance novels. Its pristine condition stood in stark contrast to its aged companions. Something about it called to her—perhaps the same instinct that had helped her survive all these years, collecting and trading the currency of secrets.

"Lilly!" Margaret Fuller's voice shattered the library's hushed atmosphere, drawing disapproving glances from the few remaining readers. The elderly woman shuffled toward the desk, her oversized purse swinging wildly and her floral scarf askew. "You'll never guess what I just heard at Mo's Diner."

Lilly straightened, a familiar warmth spreading through her chest even as shame pricked at her conscience. Margaret's visits were as reliable as clockwork, always bearing some morsel of town gossip. These moments— these small connections—were what made the endless parade of empty afternoons bearable, even if they came at the cost of others' privacy.

"Oh?" Lilly leaned forward slightly, lowering her voice

to a library-appropriate whisper. Her heart quickened with anticipation, hungry for any morsel of information that might make her feel less like an outsider looking in. "Do tell."

Margaret glanced around conspiratorially before continuing, her eyes bright with the thrill of shared secrets. "That new woman renting the cottage by the coastal path? Word is, she's not who she says she is. Left her last town in quite a hurry, and no one knows why." She leaned closer, her voice dropping further. "Jenny Wilson says she saw lights on in that cottage at all hours and heard strange noises too. Like someone pacing, maybe crying."

The information settled into Lilly's mind like a seed taking root. She'd noticed the woman—early thirties, tall, solitary, riding an old-fashioned bicycle with a basket. There was something about her that seemed...deliberate. Like someone trying very hard not to be noticed. Lilly recognized that careful invisibility; she'd perfected it over years of moving from foster home to foster home, learning to fade into the background to avoid the pain of attachment, only to be left behind anyway.

"Interesting," Lilly murmured, tapping a finger against her chin as her mind cataloged this new information. "I wonder what she's hiding."

"I suppose we'll find out soon enough," Margaret replied with a knowing smile that didn't quite reach her eyes. "Weyport has a way of revealing things, doesn't it? Just like it revealed that business with the Hendersons last summer—which we never would have known about if it weren't for you, Lilly."

'The words struck uncomfortably close to home. Twelve years in Weyport had taught her that small towns held secrets as surely as the ocean held salt. She'd made herself indispensable by knowing just enough about everyone to ensure they sought her out, shared their stories, made her feel needed. It wasn't friendship exactly, but it was better than the crushing loneliness of her early days in town, better than the hollow echo of an empty house and memories of a white dress that never made it down the aisle.

Lilly recalled that the mystery woman had appeared three days after Holbrook's environmental impact statement was quietly filed at town hall—a document Lilly had glimpsed while reshelving in the public records section. The dates nagged at her memory now, a pattern trying to emerge from chaos.

As Margaret wandered toward the fiction section, Lilly's attention returned to the mysterious diary. Her fingers traced its unmarked surface, wondering what secrets lay within its pages. Her other hand unconsciously touched her brooch.

THE AFTERNOON WORE ON, shadows lengthened across the floor as patrons gradually filtered out. Lilly moved through her usual routine with practiced efficiency

—straightening chairs, reshelving abandoned books, checking the thermostats. Her sensible brown pumps clicked softly against the hardwood floors, the sound echoing in the growing quiet. Each task was a familiar comfort, a ritual that helped keep the loneliness at bay.

Finally alone, she returned to her desk and opened the diary. The first few entries were unremarkable—daily observations, mundane details. But as she turned the pages, the tone changed. The handwriting became more urgent, less controlled, reminding her of the desperate letters she'd written to her birth mother years ago, letters that were never sent because there was no address to send them to.

One entry in particular made her breath catch:

*I tried to warn them. They wouldn't listen. Now I have no choice. If anyone finds this, know I did my best to stop it. The truth has to come out, no matter the cost. They think they've buried it deep enough, but secrets have a way of surfacing, like bodies in a flood.*

Lilly's hands trembled as she reread the words, her heart pounding against her ribs. In all her years of collecting Weyport's secrets—the affairs, the financial troubles, the family feuds—she'd never encountered anything that felt quite so...dangerous. The writer's desperation seemed to seep from the page, and for a moment she understood with perfect clarity that she'd stumbled onto something far beyond ordinary town gossip.

A sudden draft stirred the pages, drawing her attention to the windows. Outside, the coastal fog had begun its nightly advance, thick tendrils curling through the streetlights like ghostly fingers. Her beige sedan sat in its usual spot, barely visible now through the gathering gloom. The sight was familiar—she'd parked in the same place every day for twelve years—yet something about it felt different tonight. Felt wrong.

The heating system kicked on with a metallic groan, making her jump. Lilly pressed a hand to her chest, feeling the rapid flutter of her heart beneath her cardigan. The library had always been her sanctuary, the one place where being alone felt natural, even comfortable. But tonight, the rows of books seemed to loom over her, their shadows stretching like accusing fingers across the floor.

She glanced at the clock: 7:45 p.m., well past closing. She should leave and follow her usual routine, heading home to her small house with its carefully tended garden. The lavender would need watering, and her cat would be waiting for dinner. The diary could wait until morning.

Yet, something held her in place. Perhaps it was the same yearning that drove her to collect and share the town's secrets—the desperate need to matter, to be part of something larger than her solitary existence. Or perhaps it was simple curiosity, the mystery of the diary's origins too tempting to resist. After all, wasn't this what she'd always done? Used other people's stories to fill the void in her own life?

After a moment's hesitation, she slipped the diary into her bag, its weight a promise of answers to questions she hadn't yet formed. The decision felt momentous somehow, as if by taking the diary she was stepping onto a path that would change everything.

As she gathered her things, a soft thud echoed from the mezzanine above. Lilly froze, her heart suddenly racing. The sound came again, followed by the unmistakable scrape of a book being pulled from a shelf.

"Hello?" she called out, her voice steady despite her racing pulse. "We're closed."

Only silence answered, but the prickling sensation between her shoulder blades told her she wasn't alone. She turned slowly, scanning the shadows between the shelves. The security lights cast strange patterns across the floor, and for a moment she thought she saw movement near the reference section.

"Is someone there?" Her voice sounded small in the vast space.

Another sound—footsteps, soft but distinct—came from the direction of the history section. Lilly's sanctuary had become a maze of shadows and hidden threats. She backed toward her desk, one hand clutching her bag close, the other groping for the phone.

The diary rested against her hip through the fabric of her bag, suddenly heavy with the weight of whatever secrets it contained. All her years of collecting whispered conversations and traded confidences hadn't prepared her for this creeping dread, this certainty that she'd stumbled onto something far more dangerous than town gossip.

A floorboard creaked directly above her head. Lilly's breath caught in her throat as she looked up at the mezzanine's darkened outline. Someone was up there, moving with deliberate slowness, tracking her movements. The familiar walls of the library now felt like a cage, the rows of books transforming into bars that trapped her with whoever lurked in the shadows.

The fog outside swirled against the windows, thick and suffocating. Even her reliable beige sedan, barely visible through the gloom, offered little comfort. She was alone here—truly alone—with someone who didn't want to be seen.

And somehow, deep in her bones, she knew it had something to do with the diary in her bag.

# CHAPTER 2

Morning sunlight filtered through the library's tall windows, casting golden fingers across worn floorboards that had witnessed decades of Weyport's quiet dramas. Lilly stood at the circulation desk, her hands moving with practiced efficiency over returned books while her mind circled endlessly around the previous night's encounter. The leather-bound diary sat in her bottom drawer like a splinter in her conscience, its presence gnawing at her.

The familiar weight of her cardigan draped across her shoulders, a shield against more than just the autumn chill. She adjusted her reading glasses, the gold frames catching the light as she straightened a stack of novels. Everything in its place, she thought, a mantra that had carried her through countless lonely days. But now the careful order of her world felt as fragile as the leaves skittering past the windows.

The bell above the door chimed, its clear note splitting the quiet. Young Tommy Miller entered, his cheeks flushed from the morning crispness, clutching a dog-eared paperback to his chest. He disappeared into the stacks, and Lilly smiled softly at his familiar enthusiasm for books. A few minutes later, he approached the counter with both his returned book and a new selection.

"Miss Cooper, can I check this one out, please?" His eager voice carried the innocence she sometimes feared she'd lost.

Lilly's heart softened as she took both books, scanning in the return before reaching for his new choice. "Of course, Tommy. How's your mother doing?"

"She's good. Said to tell you thanks for the soup recipe. She made it last night."

A genuine smile touched Lilly's lips. "I'm glad she liked it."

As Tommy bounded away, Lilly felt a momentary warmth that quickly faded as she noticed the three women huddled around a table near the back of the library, their voices hushed but animated. She recognized them immediately: Karla Andrews, the mayor's wife, with her perfectly coiffed silver hair; Susan Bellamy, who owned the town's gift shop and collected gossip like some people collected seashells; and Evelyn Pierce, a retired school-teacher whose sharp eyes missed nothing.

Lilly lingered nearby, straightening books while straining to catch fragments of their conversation.

"Did you see how she avoided the planning commission meeting last night?" Susan's whisper barely carried. "Right after they presented that harbor expansion project."

"Of course. She knows she's in trouble," Karla replied, her voice dropping further. "And did you notice something odd about those environmental reports? Henry says the numbers don't match what we've seen in other development proposals—"

Their voices faded to unintelligible murmurs, and Lilly fought the urge to step closer. She busied herself with a nearby cart of books, her ears straining for any clear words. Suddenly, Susan's voice rose slightly, cutting through the quiet.

"Well, if she thinks she can hide it, she's wrong."

The three women froze as Lilly turned toward them, her expression carefully neutral but questioning. They briefly exchanged glances heavy with unspoken meaning.

"Morning, Lilly," Evelyn offered with artificial brightness. "Lovely day, isn't it?"

"It is," Lilly replied, her tone matching Evelyn's while her heart hammered. "Everything all right over here?"

"Oh, just catching up on books and such," Karla dismissed with a wave. "You know how it is."

Lilly nodded, maintaining her practiced smile. But as she moved away, Susan's unwelcome whispered words reached her ears, "Typical Lillian Looselips. Always has to poke her nose where it doesn't belong."

The words stung like salt in an old wound, but Lilly kept her head high as she continued her rounds. The nickname followed her like a shadow, a reminder of how the town truly saw her despite her years of service.

By midafternoon, the library had settled into its usual lull. Lilly stood at the front desk, mechanically processing returns while her mind churned with doubts. The burden of solitude pressed against her chest, as familiar as the scent of aged paper that surrounded her. She caught her reflection in the window—tired eyes staring back from behind gold-rimmed glasses, the weight of unspoken secrets visible in the shadows beneath them.

The afternoon light caught something metallic outside her window—a dark sedan parked across the street, its tinted windshield reflecting the sun at an angle that suggested its occupant was watching the library entrance. She recognized the vehicle—a black car she'd glimpsed three times in the past week, always at a careful distance. Always when she was alone.

She spent the rest of the afternoon in a daze of unease, efficiently moving through her duties while her mind raced with possibilities. The diary's presence felt like a live current, sending occasional shivers through her whenever she passed near it. Twice she caught herself reaching for the drawer handle, fingers trembling with the urge to read more, to uncover whatever dark truth lay hidden in those pages. But each time, she forced herself to withdraw, aware that the library's open spaces offered too many opportunities for prying eyes.

The afternoon light gradually shifted, painting the walls in amber and gold, transforming the familiar shelves into something almost otherworldly. Dust motes danced in the slanting rays like silent messengers, carrying secrets between shadow and light. In the reference section, Mrs. Henderson pored over old newspapers, her arthritic fingers tracing headlines from decades past. The soft rustle of pages turning, normally a comfort, now seemed to carry undertones of warning.

Lilly found herself watching the patrons more closely than usual, noting their movements, their choices, their whispered conversations. Had that man in the business suit lingered too long in periodicals? Why did the woman with the red scarf keep glancing toward the staff area? Every action seemed loaded with potential meaning, every casual gesture possibly concealing darker purpose.

The weight of the diary's presence had changed something fundamental in her relationship with the library. Where once she'd found solace in knowing everyone's secrets, now she felt the burden of carrying one that could upend everything. The very air seemed charged with possibility and threat, like the charged stillness before a storm.

Evening approached with the stealth of a rising tide. As Lilly moved through her closing routine, memories of the previous night's encounter sent shivers down her spine. The street outside had grown quiet, lampposts casting elongated shadows across empty sidewalks. She studied her reflection in the frosted glass of the library doors, noting the slight tremor in her hands as she turned the key in the lock.

Her beige sedan sat in its usual spot, a testament to her carefully ordered life. But as she walked to her car, the click of her heels echoing in the stillness, something felt off. She looked back at the library, its darkened windows staring back like empty eyes.

A movement caught her eye—a shadow shifting between the hydrangea bushes that bordered the parking lot. Her hands tightened on her bag, and the ever-present, unshakeable presence of the diary. But it was only Mrs. Henderson's cat, its eyes reflecting the streetlights like twin moons before it slipped away into the gathering night.

Her drive home followed its usual route—past the old lighthouse with its beam sweeping past empty streets, past Mo's Diner where Margaret Fuller held court over coffee and confidences, past the town hall where so many of Weyport's official secrets were filed away in manila folders and computer databases. Each landmark a chapter in the town's ongoing story, each shadow a potential hiding place for truths too dangerous to speak aloud.

The unease followed her home, settling into her bones like the autumn chill. Inside her quiet house, she placed the diary on her kitchen table, its presence demanding attention. The lavender in her garden released its evening fragrance through the open window. The supposedly calming aroma did little to ease her growing sense of dread.

As she prepared for bed, the diary's warnings echoed in her mind. Tomorrow she would have to decide what to do with its dangerous revelations. For now, she tucked it carefully into her bedside drawer, close enough to grab if needed, before switching off the lamp.

In the darkness, every creak of her old house seemed to carry meaning, every shadow a potential threat. From her bedroom window, she could see the distant beam of the lighthouse sweeping across the harbor, its rhythmic pattern usually a reassurance, but tonight seeming more like a searchlight seeking secrets in the dark. The sound of waves against the distant shore carried in the still night air, a constant whisper that seemed to echo the diary's warnings.

Her thoughts drifted to the mysterious woman on the coastal path, wondering if their stories were somehow intertwined. Two women trying to stay invisible, each carrying burdens too heavy to share. The silver leaf brooch on her nightstand caught the moonlight, casting tiny prisms on the wall that danced like fragments of scattered truth.

She thought of Susan's whispered accusation—Lillian Looselips—and the irony of it made her almost laugh. If they only knew how many secrets she'd kept buried over the years, how many confessions she'd locked away in the vault of her silence. But this secret, this diary...it felt different. Not just a secret to be kept, but a truth demanding action.

Sleep, when it finally came, was filled with dreams of footsteps in empty corridors and words that burned like fire on the page. In her dreams, the diary's pages turned themselves, revealing truths she wasn't ready to face, while shadows with familiar faces watched from the corners of her mind.

READ ON...

# MORE BOOKS BY URCELIA TEIXEIRA

*Angus Reid Mysteries series*
Jacob's Well
Daniel's Oil
Caleb's Cross
Hannah's Halo
Lilly's Vine

*Adam Cross series*
Every Good Gift
Every Good Plan
Every Good Work

*Jorja Rose trilogy*
Vengeance is Mine
Shadow of Fear
Wages of Sin

*Alex Hunt series*
The Papua Incident (FREE!)
The Rhapta Key
The Gilded Treason
The Alpha Strain
The Dauphin Deception
The Bari Bones
The Caiaphas Code

PICK A BUNDLE FOR MASSIVE SAVINGS exclusive to Urcelia
Teixeira Store subscribers!

Save up to 50% off plus get an additional 10% discount coupon.
Visit https://shop.urcelia.com

**More books coming soon! Sign up to my newsletter to be notified of new releases, giveaways and pre-release specials.**

# ABOUT THE AUTHOR

Award winning author of faith-filled Christian Suspense Thrillers that won't let you go!™

Urcelia Teixeira, writes gripping Christian mystery, thriller and suspense novels that will keep you on the edge of your seat! Firm in her Christian faith, all her books are free from profanity and unnecessary sexually suggestive scenes.

She made her writing debut in December 2017, kicking off her newly discovered author journey with her fast-paced archaeological adventure thriller novels that readers have described as 'Indiana Jones meets Lara Croft with a twist of Bourne.'

But, five novels in, and nearly eighteen months later, she had a spiritual re-awakening, and she wrote the sixth and final book in her Alex Hunt Adventure Thriller series. She now fondly refers to *The Caiaphas Code* as her redemption book. Her statement of faith. And although this series has reached multiple Amazon Bestseller lists, she took the bold step of following her true calling and switched to writing what honors her Creator: Christian Mystery and Suspense fiction.

The first book in her newly discovered genre went on to win the 2021 Illumination Awards Silver medal in the Christian Fiction category and the series reached multiple Amazon Bestseller lists!

While this success is a great honor and blessing, all glory goes to God alone who breathed every word through her!

A committed Christian for over twenty years, she now lives by the following mantra:

"I used to be a writer. Now I am a writer with a purpose!"

For more on Urcelia and her books, visit https://www.urcelia.com

To walk alongside her as she deepens her writing journey and walks with God, sign up to her Newsletter - https://newsletter.urcelia.com/signup

or

Follow her at

g  goodreads.com/urcelia_teixeira

f  facebook.com/urceliateixeira

BB bookbub.com/authors/urcelia-teixeira

a  amazon.com/author/urceliateixeira

○  instagram.com/urceliateixeira

P  pinterest.com/urcelia_teixeira

Made in the USA
Monee, IL
08 May 2025

17129858R00194